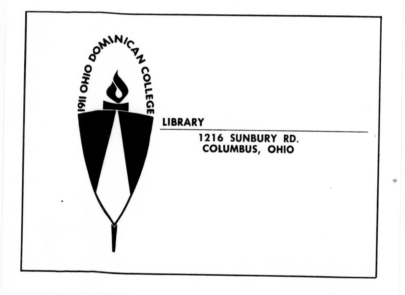

J
C

Also by Gary Crew:
STRANGE OBJECTS
NO SUCH COUNTRY

For Rebecca . . . with thanks

SIMON & SCHUSTER BOOKS FOR YOUNG READERS
An imprint of Simon & Schuster Children's Publishing Division
1230 Avenue of the Americas, New York, New York 10020

Book design by Anahid Hamparian
The text for this book is set in 12-point Bembo.
Manufactured in the United States of America
First Edition
10 9 8 7 6 5 4 3 2 1
Library of Congress Cataloging-in-Publication Data
Crew, Gary, 1947–
Angel's gate / Gary Crew.
p.   cm.
Summary: Kimmy encounters two wild children who have grown up in the hills of Australia
and tries to protect them from the unknown person who murdered their father.
ISBN 0-689-80166-1
[1. Feral children—Fiction. 2. Australia—Fiction. 3. Mystery and detective stories.] I. Title.
PZ7.C867An   1995   [Fic]—dc20   95-4047

Be not forgetful to entertain strangers:
for thereby some have entertained angels unawares.

HEBREWS 13:2

one

the night the first wild child was captured, I was woken from my sleep by the sound of car doors slamming. I opened my eyes; lights were flashing across the ceiling of my bedroom. I sat up at once, and there, holding aside the lace curtain of my window, was my sister, Julia.

"What is it?" I said.

She was staring into the yard, concentrating. She looked very beautiful; the moonlight on her face, her dark hair out and spilling down her back, her white nightdress falling in straight folds like marble.

"Julia . . ." I persisted.

"It's nothing," she said. "It's only our father come home. Go back to sleep." I knew that she was lying. If my father was called out late, he came home quietly and without lights.

I threw off my covers and slipped from the bed. Standing beside her, I looked down.

Three vehicles were parked in our yard. I could see my father's car, which was black and polished; the dull red of the Fergusons' pickup truck; and up near the house, with its doors wide open, Sergeant Mortimer's four-wheel drive. There seemed to be lights flashing everywhere and by them I could make out a woman, and several men, one of whom was my father; I could tell by his hat and his black bag. Between two of them was a smaller figure, bundled up in a rug, but walking, or being half carried, toward the door of my father's office. I knew straight away what had happened.

"They've caught one," I whispered. "Haven't they?"

Julia said nothing.

"They have, haven't they? They've got one," I said.

She took her hand from the curtain and turned away. The lace fell in front of my face, and I drew back, looking after her. At my door she stopped. "They get all of us," she said, "sooner or later." Then she vanished into the darkness of the hall.

two

We lived with our parents in Jericho, a country town that had seen better days. Our father was the doctor; our mother, whom he had met and married when they worked together during his internship in the city, was a nurse. Together they conducted a practice from rooms on the ground floor of our house, a big sandstone building called The Laurels. My parents had bought the place soon after they were married, and made it their home. Julia and I had known no other.

As my mother was a nurse, she spent much of her time in the reception room of the office and so, from hearing the gossip of the patients, she became an expert on local history. She knew, for example, that since our town was surrounded by mountains, it had been named after the walled city of Jericho in the Bible. She also learned the history of our house. It was built as a military barracks in the 1870s—more than a century ago—when the mountains round about had been overrun by gold-hungry miners who had been lured to Australia from all over the world. At that time, the cellar beneath the office had served as lockup cells for claim jumpers, drunks, and murderers. I had run my fingers over curses and prayers gouged in the walls and floor joists.

The cells had other purposes now. Sometimes, in the night, the house came alive to the hum of the gas-driven generator which operated the cold storage room installed there, and I knew that my father had laid out a corpse, an accident victim or a heart case, to be taken away in the morning.

My father worked at his hobby of taxidermy in one of these cells. Sometimes, if he couldn't hear us knocking on the door beneath the stairs, we would call to him through a little window that opened onto the yard—his only direct access to the outside world.

We hated the cellar, Julia and I.

On the ground floor of The Laurels were the rooms for my parents' medical practice and our living rooms and kitchen. There were also two smaller rooms—originally quarters for officers, my mother said—where overnight patients stayed. Sometimes there were accidents on the main road outside of town and my father would keep the injured for observation; sometimes locals were admitted for minor surgery. We might even take in a drunk, if the small police station jail was full, since all the downstairs windows were fitted with bars from the old days—except for the window into the cellar, which my father had added later, for light.

We slept above all this, my mother and father, Julia and I. My parents' and Julia's rooms were at the front of the house, facing the street. I envied Julia for having a front room; she could pull a chair up to the window, put her elbows on the sill, and see all the way down to Jericho. She could talk to whoever passed in the street. My bedroom was at the back of the house. I looked down on our yard and the old stables, now our garage. But I could go higher.

Rising from the center of the gabled roof was an observatory, accessible from the second story hall by a ladder and trapdoor in the ceiling. The observatory was a circular timber deck surrounded by an iron railing, with four iron columns that supported a bronze cupola. It was the only touch of elegance in the building but, as my mother said, it was no architectural flight of fancy: Its original function as a lookout was obvious.

I called this place "the eyrie" because only an eagle could be higher. Any day I could climb up and look out over Jericho—even as far as the Angel's Gate, the pass that broke through the smoky blue hills to the western plains beyond. Once, when I was up there, with my arms stretched out like wings in the wind, Julia looked up from the yard and saw me. She cupped her hands and yelled, "Would you fly, Kimmy? Would you be an eagle, would you?" I thought this was too stupid a question to answer and turned my wings in another direction.

When the gold fever died, the barracks was empty for years, until it was sold to the State Hospitals Authority for use as a lunatic asylum. They say that the inmates themselves built the sandstone wall that enclosed the property. This was generally believed, considering the height varied wildly, ranging from less than three feet behind our garage to over six feet near the iron gates at the front.

The name, The Laurels, came from two camphor laurel trees which had been planted in the front yard; one of these survived to our day. I suspected, judging from the size of the rotting stump and exposed roots of the other, that it had grown too big, too fast, and had threatened to knock the wall down. The surviving tree had been more fortunate—or smarter, Julia said. Although planted as close to the wall as its dead partner, this tree had grown up, not out, and now its branches arched free of the wall that stood beneath. On hot summer days I would climb up and lie in the leaf-green cool, my body flat along a scaly branch, my arms and legs dangling, like a wild boy in a picture book.

One Saturday afternoon I was lying along the laurel branch when a battered pickup truck pulled in at the curb below me. Nobody ever stopped in front of our house or approached the iron gates in the wall around our yard. Everybody seemed to know, either by hearsay or instinct, that the doctor's rooms were entered from the back of the house, off the side lane. While I watched, the front wheel of the pickup hit the curb with a jolt, and a man stepped out; a giant, red-faced, raw-boned man, dressed in the shabby clothes of a gold fossicker. These men came and went in Jericho; drifters and eccentrics, still believing that in the abandoned shafts and mines among the mountains they would find their El Dorado—or somebody else's, long since abandoned. When he left the car, heading for the gates, I saw why he had come. He walked with his right arm extended; from his elbow to his wrist it was dripping blood.

"Hey," I said, as he shook at the gate. "Hey. The entrance is at the side."

He looked up to find the voice and I dropped from the tree to the top of the wall.

"Go around," I said, pointing to the lane.

He gave me a sour look. "I want a doctor," he said.

I scrambled to the footpath. "This is the doctor's. Doctor Marriott is my father. But you can't get in that way. The gate's locked. You go around the side lane. Here . . ." I set out to lead him.

"Wait," he said and returned to the pickup. The back of the vehicle was enclosed by a canvas hood, like a covered wagon. With his good arm, he lifted a flap and muttered something—to a dog, I guessed—then he followed me.

My mother was in the kitchen, so I went straight through the reception room to the door of the examining room and knocked. The injured man stood behind me, his blood dripping onto the polished wooden floor. My father appeared and saw what was happening at once. "Get your mother," he said and called the man in with a movement of his hand. My father was never one for words.

When my mother came, she saw the dark blood on the floor. "There's something for you to do, Kim," she said. "Get the mop and bucket." She turned at the door of the examining room. "And do it properly, so nobody slips."

I was still there, dry mopping, when the man and my mother came out. His forearm was bandaged. My mother went to the reception desk, but he walked toward the door, and would have gone, except I was in his way. "Sir," she called, while he and I did an awkward two-step around the bucket and mop, "we need particulars."

He went back to the desk. She was standing there with the patients' register open in her hands.

"What?" he said.

"I need your name," she answered. "And that sort of thing."

"Flannagan," he grunted, "Paddy Flannagan."

"Patrick?" she said and he nodded.

When she leaned forward to write, I saw him look up at an eagle displayed on a stand by her desk. This was a very fine example of my father's work. It was not the giant wedge tail eagle that sometimes hung in the air above our valley, but what my father called the "little eagle"— properly known as *Hieraaetus morphnoides,* a sign on it said.

The wings of the bird spread wide as it swooped on a pop-eyed field mouse trapped forever in its talons.

My mother tolerated the eagle, but she couldn't stand to look at the specimen that my father was most proud of: His ghost bat, *Macroderma gigas,* or false vampire. This was kept in the cellar, "Exactly where it belongs," my mother said, "in the dark and out of sight."

My father's taxidermy specimens came from all over the shire, but I never saw him use an animal that had been deliberately caught.

"Your age, Mr. Flannagan?" my mother asked. "And your address?"

Flannagan turned from the eagle to face her. "Who done that bird?" he said.

"My husband," my mother answered. "The doctor."

He swung away from the desk, crossing the room in a couple of strides. At the door, he said, "Missus, you put what it cost on the slate." Then I heard his boots crunching the gravel out to the lane.

"Good riddance," my mother muttered, shutting the register. "And he can take out his own stitches. With his teeth."

But two weeks later, Flannagan turned up again.

Julia was in the backyard, waiting for her boyfriend. She was fifteen at the time, and in tenth grade—I was only in sixth—but already she had gone steady with Bobby O'Meara for two years. He was seventeen and drove a beat-up old '57 Chevy, but best of all—so far as I was concerned—Bobby helped run his parents' farm way up in the bush at a place called the North Arm. He was taking Julia there that afternoon, which was why I was buzzing around, pestering her to be allowed to go, when a pickup truck with a canvas cover turned off the side lane and stopped in our yard.

I could tell right away that it was Flannagan, but he didn't get out. He sat dead still behind the wheel, staring at us. Since I was the one who had first shown him in, and wiped up his blood, I thought it was my responsibility to do the honors. I went across to the car and stood at his window. "Good afternoon, Mr. Flannagan," I said. "How is your arm?"

I don't think he had expected me to speak. He turned away, then reached down as if he was trying to find something beneath the seat. As he leaned forward, I saw his injured arm. The bandage was gone; the remains of the stitches dangled from the weeping wound. I had been around the office long enough to recognize infection when I saw it, and was about to warn him, when the car door suddenly opened, and he towered above me.

"I came to see your father," he said, then strode off in the direction of the office, a burlap bag dangling from his hand.

"He's not there," I managed to get out, and he scowled. "It's his afternoon off. He's in the cellar. If you wait in the office, I'll get him."

I slipped past, intending to call my father through the cellar window, but my mother came to the kitchen door just as I was crouching down. "Who's that?" she said, looking toward the pickup. I told her that it was Flannagan and he wanted to see my father. She nodded. "Don't call your father," she said. "If it's those stitches he wants out, I can do that." I told her what I'd seen; she grimaced and went into the yard.

"How are you, Mr. Flannagan?" she said, walking right up to him. "And how is that arm?"

He gave her the same sour look that he had given me. Instead of returning a civil answer, he put both arms behind his back—as if to hide the injured arm and the bag. "I didn't come about the arm. I come to pay the doctor."

My mother had dealt with people like Flannagan for years. She was always kind but firm. "We aren't worried about payment, Mr. Flannagan. It's your health we're worried about. Now show me."

She stepped forward, simultaneously reaching out to touch him—or maybe lead him into the office—but he sprang back. "Leave it," he muttered. "I came to pay, then I'm gone."

From the corner of my eye I saw Julia head toward the house.

My mother held her ground. I stood behind her. "Mr. Flannagan," she said, "Kim here tells me that your arm is infected. I'd like to see if that's true. Would you . . ." She didn't finish. He pushed the injured arm at her, the wound uppermost. "There," he said. "Now you can see. I been bathing it in boiling water and salt. There ain't no infection."

I heard my mother sigh. "Mr. Flannagan . . ." she began, but before she could say more, my father appeared beside her, and Julia beside me.

"That wound's infected," my father said. "I can see that from here. Unless it's treated immediately, you risk losing your arm. Make up your mind."

Flannagan held out the bag. "I didn't come about me arm. I thought it was all right. I came to give you this. I'm scratchin' gold in the bush. I got no cash. Only this."

My father took the bag and opened it. He showed no caution. It might have been a bag full of snakes, for all he knew. I saw him start, then reach in. He took out a parrot; a blue mountain lorikeet, beautiful and very rare. The bird was dead; its head lolled sideways, its dark eyes glazed over gray. My father looked at Flannagan, then back into the bag. "There are two?"

Flannagan nodded. "I seen that stuffed eagle you done on the counter in there. I reckoned this pair would look good done up like that. I got no cash, see?"

My father's voice was so soft I could hardly hear him. "You shot these?" he asked.

Flannagan nodded again. "But there's no damage. I got them both beneath the wing. You won't see nothing when they're done."

There was silence—just for the second my father was thinking—then he held the bag out to Julia and the poor dead bird to me. "Here," he said. "Go and bury these. Your mother and I will see to this arm."

We went straight away. We knew not to hang about when our father talked quietly. We crossed the yard to the garage without saying a word. Inside, where it was dark, we looked back from behind the door. Flannagan was stamping his feet and waving his arms, but our parents were standing stock-still. Julia gave me the bag while she reached up for the garden spade, then we went out to the vegetable patch. When we looked again the three of them were gone, but the pickup truck was still there.

Julia dug the hole while I watched, holding the bag in one hand and the dead bird in the other. The soil was soft and brick red. When the hole was big enough, she stood up and put her hand out. I gave her the bird and she placed it flat in the bottom of the hole, smoothing its feathers with her fingertips. I reached into the bag and took out the second bird. It was smaller than the first and I held it across my palms. The feathers were thick and downy and blue as heaven. "Do you think they were a pair?" I said.

Julia shrugged. "Maybe. This one's not as big. Could just be younger. Like you and me."

She took the bird from me, put it in the hole next to the first, then covered them both with soil; it looked redder still against that blue. When she had finished, we put the spade away and hosed the dirt from our hands and feet. I was bending down, watching the red run between my toes, when Julia whispered, "Don't look now, but there's someone in that pickup with their eye on us."

I immediately looked at the pickup. Sure enough, the flap on the rear canopy dropped as I turned. "It's a dog," I said. "I saw Flannagan talking to it the first time he came." This was a barefaced lie, but it made me feel important. I went on with my hosing.

Julia bent down again. "Dogs have hands, do they?" she whispered. I looked back. There was nothing to see: The flap was closed; there was no movement.

"Where?" I said, lowering my head but keeping my eyes on the pickup. As I spoke, fingers appeared and the canvas was opened a little, enough for an eye to peep through.

Julia saw it too. "Wait," she whispered, and suddenly walked off toward the house.

I took my time with the hose and then, when I was certain that there was no trace of soil left on my hands, feet, arms, or legs, I turned the water off. As I did, Julia reappeared. In her hand was a pink and white peppermint stick that she had won in the lucky dip at our school fair. She winked at me, then walked straight over to the back of the pickup.

The canvas fell shut.

"Here," she said, holding out the peppermint. "Come on. I won't bite."

There was no hint of movement.

Julia stepped closer. "Come on. It's very nice. And still in its wrapper."

She moved closer again. I stood back, waiting to see. "It's peppermint," she said. "You could suck it for hours." The tip of the peppermint brushed the canvas. As we watched, a hand appeared: The fingers were small and grubby, and the fingernails were split and thick with filth. The hand came out through the flap, very slowly; then, having made contact with the candy, snatched it and withdrew. Julia looked at me and raised her eyebrows. She pulled the canvas back.

I saw two children crouching on a pile of sacks. One was a girl about fourteen or fifteen with matted, corn-colored hair hanging around her face. As for the other one—the one gnawing on the peppermint—there was no telling what it was, boy or girl; its face was like a pixie's or an elf's. It had short, wild hair sticking up all over its head. The stink coming from the sacks—or the children—was awful; I never knew whether Julia dropped the flap to avoid it, or because she had seen enough.

We had only just moved away when Flannagan appeared, followed by our mother.

". . . in a week," I heard her say, as he got into the pickup and slammed the door. Seconds later he drove away.

My mother watched him go. "That's the last we'll see of him," she said. I heard her, but I doubt that Julia did: Bobby's Chevy was waiting in the lane, its motor purring.

three

My parents didn't approve of Julia going with Bobby O'Meara. They didn't think he was right for her at all. "I didn't raise you to be running around with some lamebrained muscle-bound cow-cocky," my father told her. "And you had better get him out of your system before you go to college, I'm warning you. . . ."

My mother was kinder; she liked Bobby, but there were doubts. "Yes Julia," she would say, "I'm sure that he's always a gentleman," or "No Julia, I'm not accusing the two of you of anything, but . . ."

Julia had her own theory about why our parents didn't take to Bobby. "It's got nothing to do with him working on the farm," she said, "and nothing to do with the fact that he's a Catholic either—when did we ever go to church, for goodness sake? That's all a load of rubbish. I know what it's about; it's because he's not one of 'ours,' that's what it is. . . ."

I didn't always agree with Julia, but this time I thought she could be right. All babies delivered by our parents in the rooms at The Laurels were known familiarly as "ours"; the rest—like Bobby, who had been delivered by his sisters in a field of alfalfa—were simply "others."

In spite of my parents' objections—or maybe because of them—Julia continued to see Bobby. He came to our house on weeknights after he had finished the milking, and he and Julia would sit on the front wall and talk for hours—or until my father appeared at the door, glaring.

Sometimes Julia was allowed out to see a film at the Jericho School of Arts hall. But Saturday afternoons, when there were no patients booked, and my parents' time was taken up with other things, Bobby might come over and take us up to his farm. If this seemed likely, I would wear Julia down with begging, making promises to do her chores, anything to go with them. Whenever I was with Bobby, the world was right. He had that way about him: He was big and strong and no matter what, he was always happy.

If he took us for a drive in his Chevy and we broke down or got a flat, Bobby wouldn't make us feel miserable, like our father did; he would get out and say, "Kimbo, see up there, there's a patch of wild raspberries I reckon you should have a feed of . . . and take Jules with you. . . ." When Julia and I came back, with our lips stained red from the fruit, there he'd be with the car fixed, wiping his greasy hands on his jeans. On the way home, I'd slide down in the back seat, staring out through the smudgy window at the trees whizzing past until I nodded off and woke up in our own side lane, wondering where the afternoon had gone.

Of course, there were other times when Julia would meet Bobby in secret—using me as her cover. Not long after she started going with him, she began to visit the Jericho Public Library after school. "Be late home," she would yell airily as we left the house. "Going to the library this afternoon. Kimmy can come too." Since Julia was no student, my parents were delighted by this sudden interest in study. They had decided long before to ignore her interest in Business Studies in favor of their own ambitions for her future; at the end of the tenth grade they were sending her to the stuffy Presbyterian Ladies' High School down the coast. They no doubt considered that this extra study could only help. Besides, what harm could she come to if she was at the library with me?

After two or three of these visits I woke up to her scheme: As soon as she had chosen a book—any book, it seemed to me—we went outside and there, every time, was Bobby O'Meara's Chevy parked at the curb. "Well," Julia would say. "There's Bobby O'Meara. What a surprise." My sister was a truly accomplished liar.

I was never too sure of my fate on library afternoons. Sometimes I was allowed to go for a drive with the lovers; other times I was abandoned at the library, and told to amuse myself.

Julia knew that I loved books, and that I was on very good terms with the librarian, Miss Dunne, who wore heavy pleated skirts in any weather and twisted her hair in a tight knot at the back of her head. Miss Dunne knew our family well. Years before, when they had been cleaning out our cellars, my parents had discovered a series of very old photographs of Jericho in its gold mining heyday, and had donated them to the library. These had been framed and hung around the reading room walls. Beneath each was a plaque with the full story of the photo engraved on it. Miss Dunne was an interesting guide. Not only did she read aloud to me from each plaque, but she added her own commentary as well.

One afternoon, as I waited for Julia, Miss Dunne showed me a photo of The Laurels.

"That's your place," she said, standing beside me. "And you see that lookout at the top?" She pointed to my eyrie. "Well, there's quite a story about that; a very strange story. . . ." I knew right away that I was going to hear it, ready or not. "They say that a man threw himself off that lookout," Miss Dunne squinted at the photo, "and died."

"Really?" I gulped.

"Some time ago, Emily Pilcher expressed an interest in these pictures, and she told me the tale. I can't vouch that it's the truth, of course, but . . . well . . . who knows?"

Emily Pilcher was generally accepted as Jericho's resident loony, and had been for fifty years. Anything that she had to say—whether supported by photos or not—should be taken with several grains of salt, but I couldn't help myself. "What?" I asked. "Who knows what?"

"Emily came in here one afternoon," Miss Dunne began, "and asked to see what we had on the asylum—'The Laurels' as it is to you. Well, no doubt you know, our Emily isn't all that stable herself." Here Miss Dunne rolled her eyes wildly, then crossed them, in a truly enviable impersonation of a lunatic. "So I decided," she continued, "that I had better do what she asked, to save a scene. When the photos were produced, she studied them in great detail, then pointed to the lookout, and said, 'That's where my grandaddy died,' then she added, 'he killed a man, you know.'

"It seems that her grandfather—who was also a Pilcher—was certified insane by the doctor who superintended the place, and committed to confinement in the cellar—they had cells there then, I understand. . . ."

I understood. I remembered the curses and prayers

carved down there, and guessed now who might have made them.

". . . And would you believe, not a month had passed, than this poor Pilcher, who was out working on the wall, saw his own wife, the very woman who had sent him up for committal, trot into the grounds with the superintendent himself. That night, as the two lovers dined, talking and laughing hardly a hand's breadth above his head, Pilcher escaped from the cellar and made his way up into the house. He took a carving knife from the kitchen and drove it clear through the back of the doctor, pinning him, kicking and screaming, to the great cedar table they were eating at there."

"He murdered him?"

"In cold blood."

"And the lady?"

"Ah!" Miss Dunne rolled her eyes. "Her? Pilcher's wife? She was pregnant, you see, and spared. But Pilcher, seeing what he had done, ran up the stairs to that lookout on the roof. They say that he stood there for a minute, looking, then he leaped up onto the railing and threw himself down, bouncing once on the roof, then falling into the yard, where he broke his neck—and died."

I thanked Miss Dunne for taking the time to tell me this, and politely retreated to the foyer to wait for Julia. When I got home I hurried into the dining room. There on our cedar table—bought along with the house since it was too big to remove—was a terrible gash.

"Rubbish," Julia said when I told her the story and showed her the mark. "That's just a knot in the timber. It was there long before Emily's loony grandfather was ever thought of—and as for Miss Dunne, don't be fooled by that 'I'm just a sweet little librarian' act that she puts on; I've heard a few stories about her and what she gets up to after library hours. She lets her hair down, let me tell you."

She began to walk away, but then stopped quite suddenly. "You know, Kimmy," she said, putting her hands on her hips and looking down at me, "you're not like other boys. You're such a baby, I think you'd believe anything. Next thing we'll have *you* jumping off the roof, thinking you can fly!" Then she went upstairs, laughing.

It didn't seem so funny to me.

four

Irrespective of whether Julia believed Miss Dunne's story or not, the dining room at The Laurels was a gloomy place. We only used it for formal occasions. We preferred to eat in the big airy kitchen that opened onto the back-yard—although this openness had its disadvantages too; anybody could walk in on us while we were eating.

One night, about three or four months after our visit from Flannagan, we were having dinner when the police car pulled up in our yard. Sergeant Mortimer got out, followed by another man I hadn't seen before. When they noticed that the kitchen door was open, they came toward us. The sergeant tipped his cap.

"Evening folks," he said. "This is Tony Loutit. He's a hydrographer from up at the dam."

I sensed trouble. The construction of the Jericho dam was the biggest thing to happen in our shire since the discovery of gold—except in this case, no one was happy about it. The purpose of the dam was to supply water to the cities on the coast; but all it brought to Jericho was the flooding of our pastures and wild country and a lot of unwanted outsiders—at least, that was the local view. I chewed my food slowly, watching my father.

He got up from the table. "Evening," he said, but he didn't shake hands.

"We need some information, Doc," the sergeant began. "You know a man named Flannagan?"

"We know him. He's that gold fossicker, isn't he, Sergeant?" My mother was the one who kept information like that in her head.

"That's the one. Has he been here?"

"He has," she said. "A few months ago. He came in with a bad gash in his arm. You remember, Ivan: The one who brought the parrots."

My father nodded. "He shot two blue mountain lorikeets. He got short shrift."

"We buried them out back," I volunteered.

My father frowned and I returned my attention to my peas. "So . . ." he said, "what's his trouble?"

The sergeant tucked his cap under his arm. "Tony here has been working up at the North Arm. He came across a body in the scrub up there. We think it's Flannagan."

"Dead?" I asked, before I could stop myself.

The sergeant laughed. "Well, he's not pickin' wildflowers."

My father had heard enough. "We'll talk inside," he said, and the visitors followed him down the hall to his office.

I pushed aside my plate and got up. "I have to go to the bathroom quick," I explained, and ducked out.

I stamped as loudly as I could on the first few stairs; then, when I was satisfied they would think I had gone up, I turned back and sat on the bottom step. I could hear their voices along the hall.

". . . could it be an accident?" I heard my father say.

"I wouldn't say so," Loutit answered.

"Then are you talking about murder?"

I felt my heart beat fast.

"Doc," the sergeant said, "I wouldn't be wasting your time if this wasn't serious. Tony here has seen the body. He says it's lying on its stomach and there's a lump of wood next to it covered in . . ."

Loutit broke in. "It's a dead branch. Firewood, I reckon. There's a pile of it there. But like the sergeant says, the piece next to the body has got blood on it. . . . Look, very briefly, I was up there about an hour ago taking water level readings. I came down this logger's track and there's a pickup pulled over in a clearing. I got a surprise, I tell you—it's rough country up that way, and I've never seen anyone about before—so I got out of the truck and walked down toward the water. There's a decent stand of cedar still up there—it's a nice spot—but I looked over and saw the flies. Thousands of them. I went closer and there's a camp—a canvas lean-to and a pile of other rubbish, empty grog bottles like a pigshooter's camp. And slap bang in the middle was this body, lying flat on its face. The flies were all over it. Like a black cap, they were, all over the head."

"How do you know it was Flannagan?" my father asked.

"I'm the one who thinks it's Flannagan," the sergeant answered. "That's where his camp was, up that way. And he drives a pickup. But he's got kids, see—or he had kids at one time—and Tony here saw no sign of them."

My father gave a sort of grunt, a noise he made when he wasn't happy. "Well, Sergeant, bring him in and I'll take a look at him, if that's what you're after."

"That's what we're after all right, Doc. But I don't want to bring him in; not yet, anyway. What I'd like is for you to come out with us. Believe me, it saves a lot of trouble later if the doctor's report is based on site evidence. I've been through all this before."

"What . . . you want me up at the North Arm now? It's pitch black."

"Come on, Doc. Get your bag. I'll be waiting in the car."

Next thing, the sergeant walked straight past me. Loutit came behind him. Expecting my father to follow, I slipped behind the cellar door under the stairs.

That night I lay rigid beneath the covers listening for the throbbing of my father's car, the sound of its tires on the gravel in the yard, and finally, knowing that I would never sleep, I got up and crept down the hall.

Julia heard me and sat up.

"I can't sleep," I said.

"Well," she mumbled, "get in with me."

"I'm all right here," I said, settling in her chair by the window.

She turned over. "Good. And keep quiet."

I looked out over the wall toward the town below us. Nothing stirred; only the bright grid of streetlights showed Jericho sleeping there. Beyond stretched the wilderness, lost in blackest night.

"Jules," I whispered, unable to contain my secret any longer. "That Flannagan was murdered."

She didn't stir. "Julia. Did you hear me? Flannagan . . ."

She rolled over, adjusting her pillow so that she could see. "Who said?"

"I heard them talking in the office. He was covered in flies."

She sat up. I could see the white of her eyes.

"His head was bashed in."

"Where was he?" she said, tossing her hair back from her face.

"Up the North Arm. He had a camp up there. The man who came with the sergeant found Flannagan. He was on his face, with flies all over him. He was rotten."

"Shush," she hissed, "or they'll hear you."

I was not supposed to sleep in Julia's room. My father had caught me there before and taken me out, calling me a baby.

"He's not home yet," I reassured her. "He went with them to see the body."

She leaned forward. "Who did it? Do they know?"

I shook my head. "You remember when Flannagan came in with those children?" I heard my voice rise and tremble.

Julia threw the sheet back. "Here," she said, "get in with me."

I crawled in beside her and the sheet fell gently over me. "Could they be dead, too?" I whispered, but there was no answer.

I woke once or twice: The first time when I heard our car and later, when an engine started and puttered to a drone deep down in the cellar.

In the morning when we were at breakfast, our father came into the kitchen looking tired and irritable. He poured his tea but instead of sitting with us he took the cup and stood at the door, listening. When he seemed satisfied, he turned abruptly. "There's something in the cellar," he said to our mother over our heads. "Keep an ear open in case that generator cuts out." He kissed her on the forehead. "I've got to do those calls at the Coxes' and O'Briens'; then I'll deal with that other. . . ."

When she was sure that he had gone, Julia said, "Is it Flannagan in the cellar?"

My mother nodded. "They brought him in this morning. Your father came to bed at three, so if you know what's good for you . . ." We knew.

At school that day Julia and I were the center of attention. By morning recess there wasn't a student in the school who didn't know that a battered and bloodied body was laid out stone-cold dead in our cellar. More than once we were offered a week's pocket money for just one look, and Julia would have gone through with it too, except for fear of our father.

But the real thrill of the day came at three o'clock when we saw the Chevy parked outside the school gates. "I hear you've got a guest in your cellar," Bobby said. "I ran into Ben Cullen in town today. He's on duty up the North Arm where it happened. My dad gave me time off, and I thought you might like a drive."

Ben Cullen was a Jericho boy who had graduated from the State Police Academy and been posted home as a junior officer under Sergeant Mortimer. He was three years older than Bobby and had a bad reputation: He had the shortest temper in the shire and would let fly with his fists with very little provocation. Once, before he went down to the Academy, I saw him brought into the surgery bleeding from a deep cut over his eye. But the darkest blot against Ben Cullen was his association with a girl called Maureen Peed.

Maureen was the same age as Ben and had been in his class since first grade. Her mother had walked out years before and Maureen lived on the edge of town with her father, a produce packer at the Jericho Co-op. My mother and Julia agreed that Maureen was "plain," and anyone could see that she was overweight. To make matters worse she always wore a printed cotton skirt, with a full rope petticoat underneath, Julia said. None of these things would have made any difference to Maureen's social acceptability if she hadn't been cursed with the last name "Peed." Wherever Maureen went there was always at least one child hanging about after her—arms extended to mimic the roll of her hips and the sway of her skirt—chanting "Maureen Peed pees the bed. Maureen Peed pees the bed." I never saw Maureen react to these insults; she just went on her way.

"How can she do that?" I asked Julia after we had seen Maureen's tormentors following her one afternoon.

"How can she do what?" Julia said, being perverse.

"That! Just ignore what they're saying."

"It's in her nature."

"What?"

"She takes the line of least resistance."

"What does that mean?" I persisted.

Julia stopped and gave me one of her big-sister looks. "It means, stupid, that she's the opposite of me. Get it?" I didn't ask any more.

When Maureen finished school she took a job as a waitress at the Paradise Café. The Paradise was managed by an Aboriginal woman called Queenie Geebung, who was a great friend of my mother's. Queenie ignored the slurs against Maureen—maybe because she had suffered the same, on account of her race—so the two of them got along fine. It was Queenie who told my mother the full story about Maureen and Ben Cullen, and later my mother told it to Julia, as a warning, I suppose.

Ben first made his advances on Maureen at the Paradise. When he turned up on his leave home from the Police Academy, all spruced up in his cadet's uniform, he sometimes dropped in for a smoke with his friends. At first he paid no attention to Maureen, like everybody else, but on one of these visits he must have noticed her. "Not *her* exactly," Julia said, "but something about her; her vulnerability . . . like an animal weakened from years of wounding." After that Ben began to appear at the Paradise right on closing time, and always alone.

Four months later, when Ben had returned to the Academy, Maureen collapsed at work. Queenie recognized the signs of pregnancy and brought her to my father. When the baby was born not a word was said about it being Ben's, and since he made no move to see Maureen on his next leave—or any other—he probably never knew that it was his, though Queenie was certain.

When the baby was three months old, my father was called to the Peeds' house first thing one morning by Maureen's father. The baby was dead in its crib. There was nothing suspicious; it had simply stopped breathing. As for Maureen, some say they saw her stumbling along the highway to the coast in the early hours; some say she was sighted at the rail of the Cataract Bridge. Whichever was true, she was never seen again.

None of this had any effect on Ben Cullen. As work on the dam progressed there were plenty of new girls for him to impress, particularly when he had graduated and could strut about town in his constable's uniform with his cap tilted forward and his gun at his hip. He still had an eye for the wounded, Julia said, and just because they came from the city and were better dressed and prettier than Maureen, it didn't mean they weren't easy prey.

"Once a predator gets a taste of blood," she said, "it always goes after more. That's a basic law of nature." Julia didn't forgive easily.

So, when Bobby offered to take us to where they'd found Flannagan, Julia thought twice. "Is Ben Cullen actually on this case?" she asked.

"I don't know," Bobby said. "We were filling up with fuel and I asked him about the murder. He mentioned that he'd be up there. I just thought that you might like a quick run to check out the scene of the crime, as they say on the big screen."

Julia looked at me. It was not the sort of look that said, *Should we?* It was more, *Okay. I'm going, but not you . . .*

I felt my bottom lip tremble and before I could stop myself I was standing there blubbering.

Julia dropped her books and grabbed me by the shoulders. "Stop it," she said. "Aren't I allowed to do anything without you?"

I snivelled even louder.

"If you go," she said, "you know that you'll have nightmares for a month. Won't you? And come crawling into my bed. Won't you?" Each statement was accompanied by a shake. Even if I'd wanted to, I couldn't have answered.

Bobby came to my rescue. "Come on Jules," he coaxed, taking her hands off me. "The kid's no trouble. Just make sure that you don't get into strife with your folks, that's all."

Even though there was a new road up to the North

Arm, at least as far as the dam and across its wall, we hardly ever went that way unless Bobby took us. After the dam, the road was mostly unsealed and dangerous, with sudden hairpin bends and steep descents as it wound about the mountains. None of this worried Bobby. He tuned the radio to his favorite coastal station, gave Julia the eye and, as she slipped across the seat closer to him, took one arm from the wheel and put it around her shoulders. I sat back and looked out of the window.

The road was little more than a track cut into the side of the mountain. Its banks were thick with moss and deep green ferns whose fronds I could have reached out and touched. But I didn't. My father had told me over and over about a boy who lost his arm when he waved from the window of a train. I daren't put my arm out, though the ferns were very close.

A few miles after we had crossed the dam wall, Bobby turned off onto a bush track. I had never been out this way before and I lost my bearing until we broke free of the trees and saw some cars parked in the scrub, about one hundred yards from the water. The police four-wheel drive was there and Ben was leaning against its front fender. When we got out he sauntered over. "The sergeant's down there with the fingerprint boys from the coast. . . ." He indicated a taped-off area around a patch of taller timber almost on the water. "So you lot better piss off."

"Charming," Julia started in, but Bobby nudged her and said, "What about the kids? Any sign of them?"

Ben shrugged. "There's a search party out."

"They came to our house," I said. "And we couldn't tell . . ."

He patted me on the head. "Sure, kid. I personally haven't seen them . . . so, I wouldn't know."

"Maybe they're dead," Julia said. "Maybe they're murdered too and dumped out there. . . ."

"There's a hell of a lot of bush . . . and water," Bobby added. "Where are they looking?"

Ben raised his arm, sweeping it in an arc beginning at the camp site. "Right around the North Arm. But not as far as the Thumbs; that's too far and too wild. I told them they'd be wasting their time up that far."

Bobby looked out over the water. "You reckon? If they did—if they got into those caves—they'd be history. No one would ever find them."

"What caves?" I said.

Bobby pointed to the Thumbs, three rocky peaks protruding from the wilderness. "Way over," he said. "Those rocks are full of caves."

"Have you been there?"

"When I was a kid. Before I got stuck with the farm I was always going. It's changed a lot now, with the dam water rising. The easy way across has all gone under. But the bats are still there. See—they're coming out now."

Sure enough, far across the water I saw one, then another, and then so many dark wings beating slow and even that I couldn't even count. "They'll eat their fill tonight," he said.

I shuddered, imagining the needle sharpness of their teeth.

five

a week after the murder there were three search parties out looking for the Flannagan children. Two of these were on land; the third was a police diving team brought up from the coast. Some said that all of this was a waste of time; that there wasn't a scrap of evidence that the children had been living with Flannagan when he died. Some said that they might have been murdered—which was what Julia believed—and their bodies buried, or weighted and dropped in a backwater. Some thought they'd simply run off into the bush—but as the days passed it was generally accepted that the children wouldn't be found alive. After two weeks the search program was reduced; after three weeks it was abandoned.

There was some news: Sergeant Mortimer had managed to locate Flannagan's next of kin, his brother, who lived on a cattle property at Wintery Hill, way out past the Angel's Gate. He knew that Paddy's wife had died and left him with a daughter named Colleen, but he'd never heard of the other one. He didn't care much, either—about his brother's murder or the fate of the children—so the sergeant told my father.

We also learned a bit from Ben Cullen. For instance, he was quick to tell Bobby when fingerprints were taken from beer bottles found at the murder site, but when it came to asking him who they belonged to it was a different matter.

"Well, not bloody me," he said.

We understood from this that he knew next to nothing.

Our main informants were the patients who waited in the reception room of our father's office.

Ruby Parsons, the giantess who ran the Empire Hotel, visited the office once every two weeks for a therapeutic hip massage—a particular skill of my mother's. Ruby was a powerful woman and everyone in our house admired her—especially Julia.

On one of these visits, I heard Ruby tell about Flannagan's drinking and how he paid for it. "A good six months before he was done in," she said, lounging back on our reception settee, "that Flannagan came into my bar asking for a case of whiskey. Not a bottle, mind you, but a case! And I says to meself, now here's a bog Irish no-hoper if I ever saw one. So I says to him: 'Well then, my man, I'll show you my whiskey when you show me your money.'

"Next thing," she said, "Flannagan pulled out a bundle of grubby cloth tied up with a leather strip. He put the cloth on the bar and opened it, and when he took his hands away, there were three golden nuggets—no bigger'n match heads, mind, but gold nuggets all the same— sitting winking on the bar."

It was so long since Ruby had seen gold in Jericho, she called her man Hamish down from upstairs and others came out of the billiard room and lounge.

"I told him to get down the bank," Ruby said. "If I took that gold off him, I wouldn'ta known who I was doing in: Him or meself. 'Take it down to Harper at the bank,' I told him, 'and have it sent out and assayed proper. Then come back for the whiskey,' I said."

Flannagan swore and thumped the bar and in the end Ruby and Hamish showed him out—which would have been a sight to see, since Hamish was bigger than Ruby, who was big as a mountain.

When the children went missing it was Ruby who walked down to the police station to give the sergeant an eyewitness description of the girl.

"When Flannagan was in the gutter cursing my Hamish and calling down the wrath of every Irish saint in heaven, I see something move out of the corner of me eye and there's this girl in the front seat of a pickup parked on the road right next to me. Pretty as a picture, she was, hair yellow as corn, and blue eyes round as saucers; she sees me look and puts her hand up over her face, but I saw her clear as crystal. Then this Flannagan, when he knows that he can't get what he wants off Hamish neither, he walks off, yelling fit to kill, and gets in beside the girl and drives off, straight down Main Street all the way, straight through, outa town. But I told the sergeant she was there and I saw her plain, right beside him, before she covered her face with her hand."

Ruby was not the only person who Flannagan had tried to deal with; there were similar stories being told all over the shire, and quite a few were told directly to my mother. So, when Sergeant Mortimer finally announced that there would be an inquest into Flannagan's death— and Ben Cullen let it slip that three of the dam workers would be called to give evidence, under suspicious circumstances—the gossip rose to fever pitch.

The inquest took a month to organize. The School of Arts hall was booked, the three star witnesses were told that they were confined to the Jericho town limits, and a magistrate was organized to come up from the coast. I knew that I had no hope of going, not with permission, but the closer the day came, the more determined I was to be there—and I made arrangements to be sure of it.

The night before—when all of Jericho had heard the scandal that the magistrate was a woman, and had arrived with a man to occupy a double room at the Sovereign Hotel—I went into Julia's room to tell her my plans. She was sitting on her bed, flicking through a magazine. I sat beside her, very quietly, waiting until she had finished. When she was ready, she said, "What? Spooked so early? It's hardly dark."

"I'm not spooked," I said. "I came to tell you something. Something about tomorrow."

"What about tomorrow?"

"It's the trial . . ."

"It's not a trial, stupid, it's an inquest. Every idiot knows that. So?"

I gathered courage. "So . . . I'm going," and before I lost my nerve, I added, "Bobby said that he would help me get in."

She tilted her head this way and that. "Ooo," she breathed, shaping her mouth and making a face. "Well now. What a little schemer you are! And Bobby, too, hmm? You never know, do you?"

"I really want to go, Jules," I said, buttering her up. "I didn't say anything before because I didn't want you to tell."

She laughed and turned back to her magazine. "Why would I tell, when I'm going too?"

I couldn't believe my ears. "Julia," I said, "that's not fair.

You know that will spoil it for me. You know it will. If anyone sees you . . ."

She licked her finger and turned a page. "Julia," I tried again, but she cut me off.

"If you make plans with Bobby behind my back . . ." she pretended to give her attention to something on the page, ". . . then you can expect me to ruin them if I'm not included. So, since I'm going now, you had better fill me in."

I knew that I was trapped. Reluctantly I revealed my plan. "I was going to leave for school early, but stop at the School of Arts instead. I can wait in the bathroom there and Bobby will get me when the people have all gone in."

"Bobby again, hmm? And where did he think you would sit? On the stage?"

"In the ticket office," I said, "where I was for *Peter Pan.*"

Julia knew what I meant by that. The year before, I had been chosen to play Peter Pan in our school play and she had helped me rehearse my part. She was much better at drama than me; she had a gift for it, I thought—but when I came down with tonsillitis two days before, she'd scored the doubtful honor of being my stand-in. From the seclusion of the ticket box, where I had been allowed to sit, I had watched her bully and thump her way through the performance, while the director, the third grade teacher, Miss Fitch, sat beside me gnawing her nails and sighing, "Oh dear. Oh dear," whenever one of the Lost Boys copped a nonscripted whack from their oversized leader. This episode proved to be a source of humiliation that Julia would never forget—nor let me, either.

"Yes. I know all about you and that ticket office," she muttered.

"But if you come . . ."

"You mean, *when* I come . . ." she corrected.

"If you come it will make a fuss. The two of us. We might get caught."

She laughed. "If we take into account previous episodes, *you* are the one most likely to get caught. *You* are the one most likely to vomit or faint and draw attention to yourself. Not me." I silently acknowledged this as the truth. Then she added, under her breath, "Nobody has *ever* caught me."

"What about a note for school?" I said. This was a last-ditch stand, and halfhearted.

"If anyone asks, I'll pinch a blank medical certificate from the office and fill it in myself."

In the drawer of my father's desk was a pile of blank "sick leave" forms. My father covered these in his indecipherable scrawl if someone needed a certificate to get off work. A forgery would go undetected. Once again I was forced to admire my sister; she was always one step ahead of me.

"And yourself?" she said; she looked at me sideways, as if I hadn't thought.

"D'Arcy never asks. He'd be happy if the whole class stayed away."

Julia accepted this as a well-known fact, since Kevin D'Arcy was the most hated teacher in the Jericho school. He had taught there for twenty years, and sooner or later, every child "got" him—just as they got head lice or chicken pox—and had to put up with him for the duration.

The next morning, as planned, we turned off the main road and made a pretense of wandering carelessly down Russel Street, where the School of Arts just happened to be. There were one or two cars parked outside, among them a police car, but no people, so we slipped down the side of the building into the lopsided lavatory in the backyard. I went in first, and leaned against the wall; Julia pulled the door shut tight. "What will we do now?" I whispered. By way of an answer, she opened her school case and pulled out a magazine, then looked at me as if to say, "So, what did you bring?"

While she sat on the seat and read, I contented myself with weighing up the chances of one of the spiders on the exposed rafters above us disengaging itself from its web and dropping into my hair. Or down my back. Outside, car doors slammed from time to time which made me more nervous and fidgety, but Julia read on unconcerned, turning pages with exaggerated finger-licking intended to further annoy me.

After what seemed like hours, there was the sound of footsteps and Bobby's voice called, "Kimbo? Are you in there?"

"Yes," I whispered, "but . . ."

"I'm in here, too," Julia finished for me. "Want to join us?"

I wished that I could see his face, but he said nothing and in seconds I heard him leave.

"That'll teach him," she giggled, then went on with her reading. I watched the spiders.

Presently, I heard the footsteps again, and waited for Bobby's voice, hoping against hope that it wouldn't be someone else wanting to use the lavatory. Then he said,

"Okay. You can come out now." Stage one was over.

Julia went first, giving Bobby a long, cold stare. I followed, glad to be putting the spiders behind me. "Keep close, and hurry," he said. "There's only Ben Cullen on the door. The rest have gone in."

I didn't need an invitation, but when we went up the front stairs, and saw Ben there, leaning back on a chair with his hand on the gun holster at his belt, I thought that I would fall down dead with fear.

"What's the gun for?" I whispered to Bobby as he shoved both of us into the ticket office.

"Effect," Julia snapped, as the door closed.

The ticket office was small, but not as small as the lavatory, nor as gloomy. On a quick check, I couldn't see any spiders either. There was a bench and two windows: One that opened onto the foyer for ticket selling, and one opening into the hall. Both of these were covered by timber-slatted blinds. "You can open them a bit," I whispered to Julia. "No one will be facing this way."

"Except the magistrate and all the witnesses," she hissed.

"But we're in the dark," I insisted. "They can't see from light into dark."

She seemed to accept this as a rare demonstration of my intelligence. She pulled the blind string to open it a little and leaned forward to peer through. I could see over her shoulder. The hall was packed; all of Jericho must have been there: Shopkeepers, farmers, workers from the dam, all, like us, wanting to see and hear. I could have reached out and touched Queenie Geebung, she was so close. My mother and father were there somewhere, I knew; but nobody could see us; they were all craning forward, moving their heads this way and that to get a better view.

On the stage was a table and chair with a jug of water and a glass for the magistrate, and another chair, a little to the left, for the witnesses, I guessed.

I was disappointed with these arrangements, expecting them to be grander, and was about to say so, when Julia squeezed my arm, breathing into my ear, "If you make a single sound . . ." but before she could complete the threat, a perfectly ordinary man—with no silvery wig or black cape—appeared on stage and called very loudly, "This coroner's inquiry is in session. Coroner Crisp presiding. Be upstanding." We shrank back while the crowd got to its feet with a terrible din; then as if on cue, everyone sat again.

I heard Julia catch her breath: A woman who looked like our mother had suddenly appeared and stood behind the center table. She didn't look old or stooped or sour; nor did she wear a wig or cape. I thought that she must be a caterer going to make some announcement about lunch, but she wasn't.

"Good morning," she said. "I am Sarah Crisp, coroner for the South West Counties." There was a murmur from the crowd; she held up her hand for silence, then proceeded. "This is not a court of law. It is, as the bailiff has announced, a coroner's inquiry. It is the purpose of this inquiry to ascertain the cause of death of Patrick Flannagan, known also as Paddy Flannagan, whose body was found on the ninth of February this year. Should it be necessary to inquire into the events leading up to Flannagan's death, this will be done, and all relevant details—no matter how painful—will be established.

Furthermore, should these events suggest foul play, then matters will be turned over to criminal investigators to pursue the case. On this issue, I have been informed that two witnesses giving evidence today have already engaged legal counsel . . ." at this she turned to the left, to a group of people that I couldn't see; again the crowd murmured, and again she raised her hand, ". . . This is their right, and as it should be. Now. To begin. I call Anthony Loutit."

The bailiff repeated her call and Loutit climbed the stairs to the stage. Once he was seated, at the coroner's request, he gave a clear account of his discovery of the body. I listened hard, wondering if his story would differ from what I'd overheard at The Laurels that first night. It didn't, nor did the testimony of Sergeant Mortimer. Then my father was called—and Julia and I drew back into the gloom.

He was dressed in his gray pinstripe suit with a white shirt and blue tie. I thought that he looked very smart. In his hand he held a manila envelope of the type X rays were delivered in. It was strange to see him there. I was proud and yet afraid.

When asked, he told simply of how Loutit and the sergeant had come to our house seeking his assistance. He told of the location of the campsite and his first view of the body. He stated that Flannagan had been dead approximately eighteen to twenty-four hours before he was found by Loutit, setting the time of death at between ten P.M. February eighth and four A.M. on February ninth. All of this was reported in a calm and steady voice.

"Having ascertained that the body shown to me was in fact deceased," he said, "I acted at the direction of

Sergeant Mortimer and examined the corpse. It lay on its stomach, face downward. The earth and leaf litter around the head was stained with blood. The arms were spread wide, the legs apart; I would say there was a yard between the heels of the boots. A single wound reached from the victim's left temple to the bridge of his nose. The blow had fractured the skull causing massive and instantaneous hemorrhage which proved fatal. Subsesequent X rays support this. I am convinced that the victim died as a result of a blow from the piece of wood found beside the body. This has been referred to previously by Sergeant Mortimer." He tapped the envelope lying across his knees. "Medical documentation is here, should you wish to see it."

The coroner waved her hand. "Thank you doctor," she said. "You may step down."

He returned to his seat and she took time writing; even from where I was, I saw that she used a cheap ballpoint pen, the sort that I could buy from Frank Tassell's News and Casket for seventy cents. I wished that she had a quill that she dipped in an inkwell, or at least a fountain pen, like my father's. When she had finished, she poured water in the glass, and sipped. We waited.

"When we began," she said, "I explained that there were two purposes for this inquiry. One was to ascertain the cause of Flannagan's death; there is little doubt in my mind that this has been established. However, there was a second agenda, the logical outcome of the first: This was to establish, insofar as it was possible, the events leading up to his death, and should those events suggest foul play, to make the necessary recommendations for a criminal investigation.

"With this second purpose in mind, I ask that the following persons stand, and identify themselves: Craig Roland Van Marseveen. Adrian James Ward. Charles Stafford."

These were the witnesses we had been waiting for; the mysterious dam workers Ben Cullen had talked about. There was a general murmur, then silence. As each name was called, a man stood to face the stage.

"Thank you, gentlemen," the coroner said. "Now, which of you has legal representation here today?"

The one who answered to Van Marseveen raised his hand, and Ward, who stood beside him; then a man in a dark suit stood up—without being asked—and said, "Gregory Cleeland. I represent both Mr. Van Marseveen and Mr. Ward."

The coroner nodded and the lawyer sat down.

"Which of you will testify first?" she asked. "Mr. Van Marseveen?" When he stepped up she indicated for the others to sit, then, as he took his place on the stage, she spoke again. "Although Mr. Van Marseveen has agreed to give evidence first, I will call you both to follow him. Please note what he says carefully, so that you need not feel obliged to embellish his account—unless, of course, it differs from your own observations or opinions."

Van Marseveen was tall and thin; like most of the workers, he wore jeans and a check shirt. His stringy blond hair hung about his face, covering his eyes; he was constantly flicking his head to keep it away. When he began speaking, we couldn't hear a thing.

"I can't hear," I whispered to Julia and she jabbed me in the ribs—though I could tell that she couldn't either.

"Mr. Van Marseveen," the coroner said, "you will have to speak up if people are to hear at the back."

I felt my face turn pink; Julia muttered, "Well said," then covered her mouth, giggling.

Van Marseveen grinned at the crowd, and started again. "I first seen Paddy Flannagan about three months ago when he started coming up to the quarters. That was about December. He wasn't coming to see me, or Adrian there, or Charlie Stafford neither. He was drinking with other fellas. I saw him, but didn't take any notice. I thought he must be a new man—a worker. If he wasn't, he shouldn't have been there, not without a security pass. Then I seen that he never went out on work detail, and the only time he came around was when the booze was on—like after work. That's how we got to know him. One night we was sitting outside our cabin, and he comes over. We offered him a beer. Big mistake. He was there nearly every day after that, hanging out for more. We didn't care at first; we felt a bit sorry for him; he was a sad case. He looked like he never had a good feed. He'd been in the bush most of his life, he reckoned, and when he'd put a few beers away he was good for a yarn. But after a while he started to be a bit of a pest. We worked out that he never came for the company, just the free grog. He never brought his own and if we said—if Aidie or me said—'How about a couple on you, Paddy?' he'd say, 'I haven't been into town,' or 'It's all right for you, you got a job.' So then we wised up to him, that he was a freeloader, and told him to get lost."

"When was this?" the coroner asked.

"Middle, maybe late January. After that he never came near Aidie or me for a couple of weeks. Then one night when it was hot, we were sitting out the front of the cabin—just the two of us this night, Charlie definitely wasn't there—and Flannagan turns up and sits down on a stool right next to us, easy as you like. 'I'm not taking nothing for nothing,' he says, and next thing he sticks his hand in his pocket and takes out these little bits of gold wrapped up in a rag. Not nuggets. I wouldn't call them nuggets; they weren't much bigger than match heads. I reckon there were four or five in his hand. We had the gas light on, and they caught the light clear enough to see. Then he says, 'Ten bucks for any piece. Take your pick.' Flannagan was always after cash. Sometimes he would arrange to meet a fella in private. You know, make private sales. He'd take a man up to his camp. That camp up in the bush . . ."

At this the coroner interrupted. "Did many of the dam workers know the whereabouts of Flannagan's camp?"

"I can't say."

"What do you mean, you can't say—do you mean that you don't know? There's a big difference."

He flicked his hair. "I don't know."

"Fingerprint evidence suggests that you visited the camp. Did you?"

"Once. I went once . . . and it was just my luck that Flannagan got killed that night. Once. That's how many times I went."

"Let's move along to that occasion," she said. "To the night of the eighth of February."

"That was a Friday and straight after we knocked off, at five, we walked back into the quarters—that is, Aidie and me; it was Charlie Stafford's day off—and Aidie saw Flannagan's pickup in the parking lot. 'Look who's here,' he says; we took no notice because he hadn't been hanging around us that much. But when we got to our cabin, we heard voices. We looked at each other; Charlie was supposed to be away, but one of the voices was his. 'Charlie's got Flannagan in there,' Aidie said. When we went in, there they were sitting on Charlie's bunk. Flannagan had been drinking hard. His speech was slurred real bad. He reckoned that he had something to trade. Something special. Up at his camp. He wouldn't say what it was. Aidie and me weren't interested, but Charlie was, except he didn't want to go alone. He asked us if we'd come if he took his vehicle. So we went to keep Charlie happy. As it turned out, that was another mistake.

"We followed Flannagan's pickup out of town, across the dam wall and way up the North Arm. It was black as hell out there. None of us knew where we were going, but Charlie kept following the taillight of the pickup; he was determined to see what was offering. When the road stopped, Flannagan pulled over and we got out and went down this track into a stand of heavy forest. We lost him for a while, maybe three minutes or more, and we were calling him, then next thing he's there in front of us with a kerosene lamp, and he says 'Come on through,' and then we see the camp—this pile of rubbish and bits of tin and sheets of industrial plastic. We waited while he built up a fire, then me and Aidie sat beside it and had a few beers. Flannagan and Charlie were under a lean-to talking. Charlie didn't sound too happy, and after a while he came back to the fire, then Flannagan did too. Flannagan ignored Charlie, and started yarning with us and hitting the booze heavy. Charlie said he was going back to his car to lie down; we'd all been drinking and we let him go."

"Then you and Mr. Ward were alone with Flannagan?"

"Yes."

"For how long would you say?"

"Maybe an hour; maybe two. We were drinking. I think we both went to sleep on and off."

"We? Both? Who do you mean?"

"Aidie and me. When we got up to go Flannagan says, 'Stay. Stay,' but we never. We went up to Charlie's vehicle and got in the back."

"In the back?"

"It's a Landrover. Charlie was already asleep in the front, so we got in the back. There's a mattress. When we got in, Charlie sat up. He wanted to go then, but he couldn't find the keys. He said they must be back at the camp, so he went back down. And that was it. Me and Aidie, we went to sleep and the next thing, it was morning, and Charlie was waking us up in the parking lot at the barracks."

"You were still in the back of his vehicle?"

"Yes."

"Do you know what time it was?"

"I know exactly what time it was because Aidie looked at his watch and said it was 6:15."

"And you never saw Patrick Flannagan alive after you left him at the fire?"

"I did not. I never saw him alive after I went up to Charlie Stafford's vehicle. I'll swear to that. I'll swear on my life to that."

"Mr. Van Marseveen," she said, leaning toward him, "one last thing before you step down. We have it on good authority that Patrick Flannagan had two children. One was a girl of about fourteen; the other was possibly

46 gary crew

a boy—although we aren't certain of that. During your visit that night, did you see either of these children?"

He flicked the hair from his face, and held it back with one hand. "No, Miss. We never saw nobody except Flannagan." He looked directly at her. "Not that night." She thanked him and he stepped down.

Ward was called to testify next; he said nothing Van Marseveen hadn't already covered; then Charles Stafford, the final witness, was called.

Stafford didn't look like the average dam worker. His clothes were pressed, he wore a plain gray shirt, and ordinary trousers, not jeans. His face was different, too. The others seemed tough—tough and sly—but Charles Stafford had a pale and pudgy face; a dull face, I thought. Julia whispered, "This one's a bit of an idiot," and I nodded. He sat there, looking down at his hands folded in his lap.

"Mr. Stafford," the coroner began, "Mr. Van Marseveen has told us—and Mr. Ward has supported his account—that when they returned to your vehicle, and woke you up, you couldn't find your keys. They assume that you went back down to Flannagan's camp to find them. Is this true?"

"Yes," he said, not lifting his head.

She prompted him. "Mr. Stafford. Will you tell us what happened? What you saw there?"

He spoke like a child who has learned a part by heart. He sat up straight, and began: "I keep the keys for my Landrover on a chain with a crystal on the end. When the other two woke me up, I put my hands in my trouser pocket and the keys weren't there. I looked around on the seat and on the floor but I couldn't find them. I thought that they might have rolled out of my pocket when I sat down by the fire. I decided to go back and get them. The other two were in the back . . ."

"Wait," Miss Crisp interrupted. "I understand that you have a mattress in the back of your vehicle?"

"Yes. I go down home a lot. But I get migraine headaches and if I do I take medication and have to pull over and lie down. I can't drive when I've taken my medication. Is that all right?"

She raised her hand to say "yes."

"So I left Craig and Aidie and went down the track to the camp. I couldn't hardly see it was that dark, and when I came up close I saw the fire had died right down and Flannagan was lying there asleep, right beside it."

"Asleep? You are certain that he was asleep?"

"He was just lying there. I thought he was asleep. Why would I think anything else?"

Miss Crisp nodded. "Go on," she said.

"Well, I left him alone and looked for my keys. I turned around to the logs, where we all sat, and I looked there. But it was dark. The fire was nearly out, just glowing, not burning, so I chucked a handful of leaves on, and as soon as the flames shot up, I saw the crystal on my key ring right away. Sparkling, see, by the light of the fire." His hands were held in front of his face, moving, to demonstrate the action of the fire. He had the attention of every person in the hall. Under her breath Julia said, "If he's lying, he's a better liar than I'll ever be."

The coroner noted something on her paper, then looked up. "And what did you do after you found your keys? Did you go straight back to your vehicle?"

"Yes and no. I went up the track a bit toward the truck, but I stopped."

"Why did you do that?"

"What?"

"Why did you stop, Mr. Stafford?"

"Because I heard something. A noise, like I disturbed something. Something in the bushes. So I stopped about halfway back to the truck."

"An animal?"

"I thought it was an animal. I couldn't hardly see, like I said. The moon was blocked out by the trees. But I was sure I heard something move in the bush. Then I thought I saw something. . . ."

"But what do you mean by 'something'? Do you mean animals? Or people? What do you mean?"

"People, maybe. I thought it was Craig and Aidie. That's who I thought it might be, having a go at me, like they do. Teasing me. They do that. They like to play tricks on me and confuse me." He glanced down at the two men in the front row. "Well, sometimes they do. They don't mean any harm by it. It's only in fun. . . ."

"And was it them, Mr. Stafford?" Miss Crisp was moving him along.

"I called out to them. I called out their names. But nobody answered and when I got back to the truck, there they were, sound asleep in the back."

"You're certain that it wasn't them? Couldn't they have been down there in the bush and beaten you back to the vehicle? Mightn't they be pretending to sleep? Playing one of their jokes?"

"Yes, they could have gone down," he said, "but they'd have had to be fast. They'd have had to be very fast, since I ran all the way back myself."

"Well," she continued, "if it wasn't them, might it have

been an animal? You haven't answered that."

"Well, it might have been an animal. But I don't think so. I couldn't say. Not for sure. Not with any certainty . . . except . . ."

"Except what, Mr. Stafford?"

"Except what I saw—just for a second, mind you, and it was dark—well—seemed to run bent over . . ."

"The children," I whispered.

"Mr. Stafford, the thing or things that you saw, might they have been children? Children running?"

He gave this some thought. "Running bent over?"

"Yes, Mr. Stafford; children running bent over."

He shook his head. "No. I don't think so. Kids never run away from me. . . ."

Much later, when the crowd had left, Bobby rescued us from the ticket box and took us up to his farm. At three o'clock, when school was out, he dropped us back at Queenie's café for a malted.

After dinner that night my mother said, "You're a funny pair. I thought that you'd have a hundred questions about the Flannagan inquest, and I haven't heard one."

"Mom," Julia said, as calm as you like, "don't you think Queenie's already told us?"

"Queenie told you? When?"

"This afternoon, when we went into the Paradise for a malted."

"What did she say?"

"She said there was insufficient evidence to proceed to trial. . . ." which was the truth; but the fact that we knew it had nothing to do with Queenie.

six

I can't say with any certainty what came first—the reports of sightings of Flannagan's children or the reports of the robberies they were thought to have committed. But in the weeks and months following the inquest every second person who came into the office seemed to have a story to tell: An orchard raided, cows gone off their milk, the sound of footsteps in the shadows beneath a window . . . and every night I crept in with Julia.

One Saturday morning when my mother was in the office, I went down to ask her to help me with my homework. D'Arcy may not have cared whether we attended school or not, but he was crazy about homework; I guess because he enjoyed watching children suffer. I sat perched on a stool at my mother's elbow with my books spread out over her desk, but just as we were about to begin, our gardening man, Pa Cossey, came in.

Pa had a place on the North Arm road, not too far from the dam wall. From as early as I could remember he had lived there with his wife, who we called Ma Cossey, although neither she nor Pa was related to us. Together they had kept a cherry orchard, not a big place, but producing enough to keep them happy—until the dam went up and most of their land was lost. Maybe as a result of this—no one would ever know for sure—Ma's heart started playing up and she passed away in one of our rooms at The Laurels. I was sitting with Pa in the reception room when my father came out and told him. Not long after, Pa asked if he could do our yard—which nobody at our place ever touched—to help "get his mind off things," he said.

Pa was old and thin, with a stubbly gray beard and watery blue eyes. Whenever he came in he brought something for me, some special present. If I was at school, my mother would take it from him and leave it in my room. He liked to make things: Tiny baskets cut from the shells of candlenuts that he picked from his own tree, animals carved out of sun-hardened soap. He was an expert at "fiddly jobs," as my mother called them, like replacing glass in a broken window after a storm blew in from the hills. Once he made me a canoe from the seed pod of a Crow's Ash tree, with a little mast and a sail of bark. I floated this canoe in my bath, but when it capsized the sail came away and it was ruined. The next time Pa came in he sat with me at the kitchen table to fix it. As he worked, the tip of his tongue protruded and bubbles of saliva formed in the corners of his mouth. I waited for them to burst and dribble onto the table, but they never did—every so often he breathed in, sucking them back, and the process began again.

That particular Saturday Pa winked at my mother, then undid the pocket of his shirt. "Here," he said, reaching in and taking out a little cardboard box. "Here's something for you."

As soon as I took it I heard a hissing sound, like the steam from a boiling kettle. I opened the lid carefully. Inside was an enormous black beetle, an elephant beetle, alive and very angry, its pincers opening and closing as it tried to disentangle itself from the layer of dried leaves which lined the box.

When Pa showed me how to pick it up by holding it behind the head, I took it back to my mother's desk and half listened to their talk while I made walls and barricades from pencils and pens, leading the poor thing up blind alleys and into dead ends until it sat down flat, its legs folded beneath it, refusing to budge. I poked and prodded and finally turned my attention to Pa, whose conversation with my mother had suddenly grown interesting.

"I've had trouble every night for the last two weeks," he was saying, "and you know, I'm not sure that it's foxes. First there was the dog growling and carrying on, then the chickens squawking. I thought foxes, straight off, and went out a few times, but in the morning, I saw it wasn't foxes. Foxes can't stand up on their hind legs and undo the latch on my henhouse. Foxes go under the wire and grab a chicken there and then. There's always feathers and blood with foxes. And foxes don't take eggs either. I've known foxes to eat eggs, in hard times, in drought times when there's nothing else about, but foxes don't *take* eggs—and I've got no eggs off the chickens for a week. No. There's something else out there. Something else again."

I felt my tongue dry up in my mouth. "What?" I said, but my mother heard the fear in my voice.

"Go on, Kimmy," she said. "Take your beetle and go or you'll be having nightmares."

I heard another story one Sunday afternoon when Bobby and Julia and I stopped in at the Paradise for a malted. Bobby and Julia always had chocolate; my choice was lime, which I didn't especially like, since it was green and sickly, but it sounded adult when I ordered it.

Queenie took our orders, but didn't smile or say a single word, which was unusual and a bad sign.

"She's not happy at all," Bobby said, and right then Queenie's husband Eddie came in. He knew Bobby well, and always stopped to talk to him, but this time he walked past us and called Queenie over. She left our malteds in the mixer while the two of them went to the back of the room. I was in a cubicle facing them so I could see what was going on. Eddie was telling her something that she didn't want to hear. She covered her ears, saying, "No, no." When he left, walking past us again, Queenie ran after him onto the street. We could hear them from where we were, still waiting for our drinks.

As usual, Julia did something about it. "If they're going to fight all morning," she said, getting up, "then I'll be the waitress myself."

When Queenie came back I could tell that she'd been crying. She went straight to the back of the room again where she lit a cigarette and sat talking to herself; she didn't appear to notice that we had half finished the drinks she'd forgotten to serve. Julia saw me staring and kicked me beneath the table. "Mind your own business," she said; then she got up and went over to Queenie.

I kept my head down, working my straw to slurp the dregs from the bottom of my drink, but at the same time I observed. Though I couldn't hear a word that was said, I guessed from the movement of Queenie's hands and Julia's nodding head that she had settled down. Soon she was laughing, and Julia came back. "Okay," she said. "Let's go." We followed her out into the street.

Later, in the car, she told Bobby what had happened. In situations such as these, I lay low. If I'd asked her what Queenie said myself, she'd have said, "Nothing," and so I pretended to be sleeping. First I yawned and sighed, which I had down to a fine art, and finally I curled up on the back seat with my eyes closed and my ears open.

In no time Julia began—and for weeks afterward, I regretted that I'd heard.

"What's a Yarama?" she said. "Eddie got Queenie stirred up about a Yarama."

"A Yarama? It's a monster. An Aboriginal blood monster."

What Bobby didn't know about Aborigines wasn't worth knowing; he'd spent a lot of time hanging around with Queenie's brothers and Eddie and his pals. "It lives in the trees and drops down on its prey to suck the blood."

"That makes sense," Julia said, and told Queenie's story. The night before, Queenie and Eddie had gone down to the dam for a family get-together. Queenie had more relations than anyone I knew and this time even more had come in from out west. They set up at a place called the Flat, a broad sweep of open bush that jutted out into the dam. But when the men started drinking and the drinking led to brawling, the women took one of the cars and left. They drove farther around the dam to Fig Tree Pocket, where there was a stretch of sand and a clump of giant Moreton Bay fig trees spread wide over a clearing. The women had made a fire and settled down for a talk while the kids went for a night swim, when someone thought there was movement overhead, in the branches of a fig. Thinking it was a possum, one of the women called the kids for a possum hunt, which was something they loved, especially at night, and in trees that were as easy to climb as these. But when the kids were about to go up, the movement came again—and this time they all saw. Whatever it was, it was too big for a possum. Before anyone could stop him, one of the boys grabbed a rock and chucked it up into the branches. There was a cry, not like any animal cry they knew, and the thing leaped from branch to branch, tried to cross from one tree to another, then fell into the clearing, nearly into their fire. Queenie said that it was white and ran on all fours. The children were crying, terrified, and the women bundled them into the car and took them back to the men.

This was not the best idea; they should have packed up and gone home, Queenie said, since the men were all drunk and laughed at the story. But when Queenie made them listen Eddie stopped laughing and went back to the figs with his brother. They found tracks in the leaf litter where the thing had taken off into the bush and farther on, where it had picked up a trail that led into the hills, into the bush above the North Arm.

I listened to this with mounting terror.

That morning, when Queenie had gone into the café, sick and afraid, Eddie returned to the clearing. This time, he said, he found bones and chicken feathers, splattered with blood. Although he searched along the track, he wouldn't climb into the trees; any one of them might be the home of a Yarama, the worst of spirits. He was worried that the children had been seen by the thing, and worse, thrown a stone at it, and he came in to tell Queenie what had to be done. He and his brother were going back that night to open their veins and splatter their blood on the ground where the thing hunted, hoping that it would come down and feed on their strength—not the children's—and be satisfied.

I waited for Bobby's response but heard nothing. I opened my eyes a fraction; Julia was watching him, waiting too. "Well?" she demanded.

"What do you want me to say?"

"Queenie says they'll cut themselves. They'll slash their arms and chests. Like . . ."

"Like savages?" he said. "Is that what you were going to say?" He shook his head. "You have to learn, Jules. That's what they believe."

"Well I think it's rubbish," she muttered. Then added, turning to look at him, "You sound as if you believe it too." He watched the road ahead.

The stories I heard at school didn't make me feel any better. At morning break I'd sit beneath the school building with the farm kids—the Ballantynes, the Lawsons, the Hogans, and some of Bobby's cousins: The O'Meara gang. Most of them lived on farms bordering the dam or in the hills. They were tough kids, like Bobby, who were up at four every morning to do the cows and had to catch the early bus home every afternoon to be in time for the milking. They never talked much, but they were good friends, and good fighters too if they were pushed. I preferred them to the town kids—the Townies, as they were called—like the Harpers, De Witts, and Parkers whose parents owned shops or businesses or worked in the banks.

The boy I especially liked was Keithy Ferguson. He was a bush kid, but not wild. Keithy's mom and dad had a farm not far from Pa Cossey's, except not so much of their land had gone under.

One morning when D'Arcy had filled the blackboard with math problems that none of us could do (how much rainwater did it take to fill a tank of such and such diameter and such and such a depth if it flowed through a pipe of such and such diameter at such and such a rate), Keithy Ferguson suddenly appeared at the door, over an hour late. D'Arcy might not have cared whether we went to school or not (he never did ask where I was on the day of the inquest) but he was a stickler for punctuality. When Keithy appeared with his schoolbag in one hand and his sandwiches in the other, D'Arcy was onto him.

First he looked up at the schoolroom clock, then down at the watch on his wrist. He wanted to make it known that he was sure. "It's five minutes before the hour," he said. "You're fifty-five minutes late."

He knew that Keithy was a farm kid and that farm kids' lives were run by watches without hands—by animals and crops and weather—but he chose to show no mercy.

"It was our cows, Sir," Keithy began. "This morning they went dry . . ."

He was not allowed to finish. "I'm not interested in cows, boy," D'Arcy bellowed. "I'm interested in education. And if your parents cared as much about your future as they did about their cows then you'd be a better person for it. Get to your seat."

Keithy knew that his parents' farm *was* his future, but

he said nothing, like many country people, and did his best to solve the set problem, though D'Arcy picked on him and riled him until lunch time.

When he finally joined us on the benches where we ate, Keithy was the center of attention.

"D'Arcy's a bastard," someone said.

"A bloody bastard," someone else added.

I would have liked to say that, but swearing was strictly forbidden by my father and I lived my life convinced that wherever I was, he could hear me. I said, "It's terrible when you get into trouble for telling the truth."

This simple statement seemed to impress Keithy more than any swear word. "Yes," he agreed, giving me a serious look. "I only told him what my father told me to."

There was something in his voice that caused a stir among the group. As one, we looked at him, our sandwiches caught midway to our mouths.

"What does that mean?" someone said.

Keithy was a quiet boy, never one to make a fuss, but this morning he had a good story to tell and an audience primed to listen.

"What I meant," he said, taking another bite from his sandwich to give him the stamina to continue, "was that I didn't lie. My father said, 'Tell that bugger D'Arcy our cows went dry,' and I did. That was exactly what I said."

A murmur of agreement ran around the group.

Andrew Ballantyne leaned forward. "But you didn't say why they went dry, hey?"

"No," Keithy agreed, "but I'll tell you now if you like."

Our silence was taken as assent. "We were asleep, Mom and Dad and me, when our dog put on a terrible turn from out in the shed. Barking and barking. I heard

Dad's bedsprings go, and then I heard him get up and go out. He yelled at Blue but he kept on barking so I got up too, and my mother. Dad was outside in the yard—I could see his pajamas plain as day. I called out 'Can you see anything?' but he shook his head. Then when the dog kept on and on, Dad went down toward the tractor shed.

"I came out into the yard after him and when I did, I saw something moving down by the cow bails, something white, like a person bent over, or crouched down . . ."

I felt my stomach turn.

". . . Then I saw another shape, the same, but bigger. It was behind the first one, following it I reckon. They were coming out of the bails and across the milking yard, and when I saw the second one, I yelled out to Dad and he came running. Just when he got to me in the middle of the yard, I saw them again and pointed without making a sound. Dad saw them too, right behind the bails. He let out a yell but it was a mistake. They took off, not running on the ground, but just above, all light and white . . ." His voice dropped to a whisper, ". . . like ghosts."

The silence that followed was so awful he seemed surprised. "That's how come we got no milk. See?"

I saw all right. . . . Night after night as my curtains rose and fell on the breeze off the hills, all sorts of apparitions floated into my room to haunt me. And then, one rain-lashed night in early spring, a "wild child" finally separated itself from the darkness and stood before me.

seven

On the first Saturday of September every year the Jericho District Spring Dance was held in the old Rural Youth hall at Winch's Crossing, a run-down hamlet on the far side of the dam. Locals considered the Spring Dance to be the highlight of Jericho's social calendar and by August, discussion about dance preparations had almost overtaken the rumors of sighting the wild children.

From all the talk in our reception room, I understood that the dance was pretty much a country and western affair, so I was surprised to hear that Julia wanted to go, and even more surprised to see pictures of evening dresses and ball gowns cut from flash fashion magazines appearing on the walls of her bedroom.

One morning when she had got out of bed before me, I asked, "Julia, do you think they're the sort of dresses that they'd wear to the Spring Dance?"

She was sitting at her dresser brushing her hair, and looked at me in the mirror. "What's that supposed to mean?" she said, holding her brush steady until I answered.

One look at her expression and I knew that I was entering dangerous territory. I thought fast. "I mean, aren't all those dresses a bit good for that dance? Won't the others wear jeans or square-dance stuff?"

Julia sneered and resumed her brushing. "I hope they do . . . which is exactly why I'm going . . . and wearing one of those . . ." she nodded toward the pictures on the wall.

Two weeks before the dance my mother took Julia to buy her dress. There was nothing that suited in Jericho, so they caught the bus down to the big stores at the coast. I was left at home with my father. This proved to be one of the longest days of my life and I spent half of it sitting in my tree watching the road. When they finally came home, I slipped down onto the wall, waving, and to my surprise Julia waved back. Julia rarely showed any signs of happiness, but that afternoon as she carried the dress box in—done up with red and white ribbon as it was—she was all smiles. My mother was pleased too and announced that after dinner, when my father was ready, Julia would show us the dress.

My father and I waited in the living room. He sat reading and I lay on the floor working at a drawing I had begun that day. I thought, *she must come down soon,* but it seemed hours before I heard the sound of high heels tapping along the hall above. My father heard too, and watched the stairs. I suppose that he had some expectation of how Julia would look, that the dress would be pink and pretty with puffy sleeves.

The first thing we saw were her shoes. They were silver, with high heels and a flash of something sparkling at the side. Then came her legs, bare to well above the knee, then the dress, bright red, shiny, and very short. Very, very short. And tight fitted. "A sheath," she called it later; skin tight across her stomach and cut low, revealing the beginnings of her breasts. And since her dark hair was up, pinned somehow at the back of her head, her neck and shoulders were exposed.

She stopped on the stairs, then turned to face us. I looked at my father. I saw a muscle tighten in his neck, tight as a wire.

"Take that off," he said, his voice even and soft. "You won't be wearing that."

The smile died on Julia's lips and she lifted her hand to grip the balustrade.

My mother came down behind her. "Ivan," she said. My father had returned to his reading. "Ivan," she repeated. This time her voice was more demanding and he looked up. "I was with Julia when she chose this dress. It won't be going back."

No more was said about the red dress in my hearing, though there followed many sessions behind closed doors before the night of the dance.

When Julia finally appeared, ready to leave, a compromise had been reached: She was wearing the dress, but covering the top—the part that most offended, I was told—she wore a little jacket of white lace.

The night was humid with a storm threatening. Bobby arrived in a hired suit and while we waited for Julia, I talked to him out in the yard.

"It's only a bush dance," he complained. "I could easily have gone in my jeans."

I thought that he looked smart, particularly in the red bow tie and cummerbund that Julia had chosen to match her dress.

"I tell you," he said, "this is the last time she makes a monkey out of me, dressed up like I'm going to the Ritz."

My father's conditions were that Bobby was allowed

to take Julia but not bring her home—he would do that himself. The trouble this caused might not have been as dramatic as the episode with the dress, but it went on longer and was more out in the open.

"What are you trying to say?" I heard Julia yell at my father. "That he could only 'have his way with me' coming home? That he wouldn't do anything on the way? Is that it? Is that what you're trying to say?"

He refused to answer.

"So," she went on just as loudly, "do you think that people only have sex after dark? Or at the full moon like werewolves?"

There was no werewolf moon that night. A storm blew in through the Angel's Gate and squall after squall lashed the front of the house until it shuddered from cellar to roof. I couldn't sleep and my mother found me by the window in Julia's room, watching the lightning fire the sky over Jericho.

"Get away from there," she said, coming in and shutting the curtains. "That glass could blow in anytime, and what would happen then?"

She took me by the elbow and sat down beside me on the bed. "Now," she said, changing her tone, "I want you to do me a favor."

"What?" I said, pulling away and seriously considering sulking.

"I want you to get a jacket and a cap and go with your father to pick up Julia."

I could hardly believe my ears. Me? Go out on a night like this? Through the bush to Winch's Crossing? "But you just told me . . ."

"Kim," she said, getting up, "I've got an emergency downstairs with Mrs. Titlow and the last thing I need is an argument with you. If this storm gets any worse and we lose power, someone has to be here to start the generator—besides, I don't want any more trouble between your father and Julia."

"But . . ." I tried again.

"Please," she coaxed. "I know it's a terrible night. Do it for your sister."

My father drove at a snail's pace at the best of times but that night he was slower than ever, hunched over the steering wheel, peering over the top of his glasses. We twisted and turned through the valleys with the wind howling down from the hills and the rain lashing against the windshield. Apart from the orders he gave me—by a grunt or sign—to wipe our steaming breath from the misted glass, we didn't speak.

At last I saw the warm yellow lights of the hall, and when we stopped in front of it I searched for Julia and Bobby among the crowd huddled on the porch. Even with the window up and the din of the rain, I could hear the sound of the band and the stamping of the dancers' feet.

"Can you see them?" my father said.

I shook my head. He sounded the horn impatiently but with all the noise nobody would have heard.

"I'll go in," I said, and got out before he could stop me. It was better than sitting there watching him get angrier and angrier.

I pulled my cap down and made a run for the porch, dodging puddles as I went. When I reached the stairs there were cries of "Gangway," and "Let the kid through," and the crowd parted, letting me see inside.

Chinese lanterns dangled from the rafters, their patterned paper shades lit from within by fiery bulbs. Above every door hung festoons of bright bunting, and paper streamers of springtime green and gold twisted and stretched from window to window across the width of the hall.

I could see no sign of Julia or Bobby among the sea of bodies and I realized that I had to do something or get caught up in the dance myself. I edged around the wall, peering between the dancers. At the front of the hall I saw Queenie standing behind a picnic table, guarding the punch bowl. She saw me, too, and dragged me behind the table away from the crowd.

"Queenie," I shouted, "have you seen Julia?"

She shook her head. "Big fight," she shouted back. "Her and Bobby had a big fight."

"A fight?" I repeated.

In answer she pointed to the dance floor. There was Bobby coming toward me in some sort of progressive barn dance. His suit coat and bow tie were gone, and the bright red cummerbund was now tied around his head, pirate fashion. He was having a great time.

I stepped out onto the floor but although he saw me, he couldn't stop. "Come on, Kimbo," he yelled. "Keep up!"

I did my best. Ducking and swerving I ran alongside.

"My father's here for Julia," I said.

"We had a fight," he answered. "I had a drink with that Van Marseveen . . . and she cracked up . . . bad company, she reckoned."

"Where is she now?"

"Out the back . . . see . . ."

Somehow he managed to free one arm long enough to point in the direction of the back door. I nodded and fought my way over. The door was partly open, and before I even reached it I saw a leg and a silver shoe. She was standing under an awning at the top of the stairs watching the rain.

"Thank goodness," she said when she saw me. "I've been waiting for you."

"Well, why aren't you out the front? How did you expect us to find you back here?"

She raised her eyebrows. "I'm not standing out there with that lot—I've already had a go at Bobby about that. He was drinking with that Van Marseveen, from the inquest. . . ."

I couldn't be bothered listening to her. "You have to come now," I said, "or else we'll both be in trouble. . . ." and I turned toward the door; but as I did, she pulled off her shoes and started down the stairs.

"This way," she said. "It's faster."

"Julia," I called, "Julia!" but I heard her laughing as she ran through the rain below me. Like an idiot I followed.

We were both drenched by the time we tumbled into the car and, without waiting for explanations, my father started up and drove off. Before he had gone ten yards, there was a knock on the window and Bobby's face appeared at the glass; his hair dripping wet, like ours, the red cummerbund plastered against his neck.

"I'll call you," he was saying, "I'll call you," then my father accelerated and he was gone.

Julia was very excited. She leaned over the back of the seat and went on and on with stories about the terrible dresses and the stupid dances and the awful music, but never once did she mention the fight or the fact that she had spent half her time alone on the back stairs.

All the while she gabbled on, her sodden hair was dripping onto my father's shoulder; but as we dipped toward the Rapids Bridge, which was low and treacherous even in good weather, she had the sense to be quiet and I looked down at the fury of wild water that raged below us. We climbed, still in silence, out of the natural declivity that formed the riverbed and into the thickest of the North Arm bush, a patch of forest so dense that the storm seemed unable to penetrate and the road appeared bone-dry. As the wipers swept the last of the rain from the windshield, our headlights caught something, a creature, crouched in the center of the road.

There was no screeching halt, no panic, but something almost polite, somehow decent and civilized, about the way my father brought the car to a stop.

The thing stood and turned to face us. It wore trousers, or what remained of trousers. As we sat staring, it raised one hand to protect its eyes from the glare of the headlights. The other hand hung at its side, gripping the limp body of a hare. Then, without any sign of urgency or fear, it stepped out of the light and vanished into the darkness of the forest. We had disturbed it feeding.

"What was that?" was all my father could manage.

"The Flannagan kid," Julia breathed against my ear.

I saw it was a boy, a terrible, wild boy.

Later we sat in the kitchen and told our mother the stories. Julia went first, telling over again her particular version of what had happened at the dance. I was allowed exclusive rights to the episode with the boy on the road. But when it came time for bed, Julia cried out in horror: Maybe it was the rain, maybe her own perspiration, but the lace jacket was no longer white. Beneath the sleeves and down the center of the back it was stained red, the color of her dress, the color of blood.

eight

late one Sunday afternoon a few weeks after the Spring Dance, my mother called Julia and me down to the kitchen to help prepare a baked dinner. My job was to shell the peas. Julia was supposed to be peeling the potatoes, but since she hadn't heard from Bobby all day, most of her energy was taken up with grunting and snarling, until he appeared at the door. He was grinning from ear to ear.

"I saw the doctor was out," he said, indicating the empty driveway, "so I thought it would be all right to come over . . . is it?" He directed this at my mother, who smiled and called him in.

Julia pushed back her chair, bumping the table and spilling the peas onto the floor. "Where have you been?" she started in. "I was ringing you all morning. Why didn't you say that you were coming?"

She went to shake him, to give him a good teeth rattler like the ones she gave me, but he guessed her intention and skipped away, his hands behind his back. When he had skirted the table to stand in the protection of my mother, he caught his breath and said, "Who says I came to see you anyway?"

This stopped Julia in her tracks. "Oh," she said. "Did you come to see Mom then?" This was possible. Without her permission, Bobby wouldn't have been allowed anywhere near our house.

"No," he said, "and not you either. This time I came to see Kimbo." As he spoke he brought his hands out from behind his back to offer me a plastic lunch box.

I sat there gaping.

"Well?" he said, "do you want it, or should I give it to Miss Cranky here?" He nodded toward Julia, who stood to one side with her hands on her hips.

"What is it?" I said, getting up and reaching out.

He shook his head. "I'm not saying. Open it. You'll see."

I took the box and put it on the table. It was smeared with mud. When I opened it I saw that the inside was stuffed with matted grass. Judging by the presents that I got from Pa, this would be to protect a living thing: A penny turtle, maybe, or a lizard. But as I sorted through the grass I couldn't find a thing, except for a few flat, red stones which I took out and put on the table. When I had finally reached the bottom and saw that there was nothing else, I started to feel uneasy, suspecting that I had been tricked. I felt the tears start and wasn't game to look up.

"What's supposed to be in here?" I said.

Bobby reached over and picked up one of the stones. "Watch," he said. He held the stone flat in his palm, spat on it, rubbed the saliva with his finger, then wiped it clean on his jeans. "Now look." He held the stone out for us. Impressed in the surface was the shape of a shell. "It's a fossil. Millions of years old. Here. I'll show you." He picked up a handful of the stones and took them to the sink where he rinsed them. He came back, shaking them dry.

"See," he said, "they're all the same. . . ." On each stone

was the impression of a shell, or more than one. "I found them all together. . . ."

"Where?" Julia demanded, flopping into a chair. "That's what I'd like to know."

"Am I in trouble because I went somewhere without your approval?" he said, attempting to give her a hug.

She shook him off and he turned away toward the door.

Seeing an argument developing, my mother made some excuse to leave the room. I took the hint, thanked Bobby for the fossils, then gathered them into the lunch box. "I'll wash these under the hose in the yard," I said, going out the door. "I'll talk to you later, Bobby."

"Hey," he called, coming after me, "when's your dad coming home?"

This was a question that none of us could ever answer with any accuracy. "I don't know," I admitted, unrolling the hose. "It depends on the patient and how far he has to go." He seemed to accept that and went back into the kitchen.

In no time I had the stones clean enough to see every detail of the fossils. When I'd finished, I went down to the shed and got some old newspapers. I spread these out on the back step, then started putting the stones on them to dry. Bobby and Julia were still inside talking, but I was too busy to take any notice of them until I heard Bobby say Ben Cullen's name—which gave me a reason to listen.

"I'm not blaming Ben," he said. "If you would just shut up for a minute . . ."

She said something that I couldn't hear; something smart, I'd say, but after that she was quiet and I heard the peas rattling into the bowl. Then he started speaking again. He was explaining something that happened the night before, when they had been to a movie at the School of Arts hall. "After I dropped you," he said, "I didn't go home the usual way. When I got through town I thought, *It's a nice night. There's a full moon. The Chevy's purring. Why not take the old Bella Vista road and have a look at the dam from there?* It was beautiful. The surface of the water was silver, clear down to the Cataract Bridge . . . I thought about you when I was up there, Jules."

Julia cut in, but he went on.

"I know, I'm sorry. If it wasn't so late, I would have come back and got you, okay? So I was thinking I'd go on home, but when I got out near Taylor's, around the bends there . . ."

I knew Taylor's; it was a lonely place.

". . . I ran slap bang into a detour sign—it looks like they're putting in a culvert to take runoff from the dam. I had to swing hard to the right on a side track, rough as guts, and all of a sudden, this car came out of the scrub, straight at me. It didn't have a single light on, even way out there. I threw the wheel over and got out of his way, but as he went past I saw that it was Ben in the police Landrover. He put his hand up to shield his face from my lights but I could see that it was him. I stopped right there, thinking that he had seen me and would stop too, but he didn't. Once he got back on the track he gunned it toward town, still without lights. I sat for a minute to steady myself, then I went on home, but all the way I couldn't help wondering what it was that he was doing out there at that time of night. And there was something else. It wasn't just that he put his arm up when he saw me coming, it was more than that. For a second it looked like he took his other hand off the wheel as well, and pushed something back against the seat—and Jules, I swear it was a rifle.

"I went down this morning and did the cows with Dad, then I took the milk into the depot. Mom had asked me to pick up an order at the co-op, so I dropped in there too. The Landrover was parked outside, covered in mud, and just as I got to the door Ben came out, lighting a smoke. I thought, *Play it safe,* so I said, 'I didn't see you in town last night.'

"He shrugged and sidestepped me to get to the car, but when he was getting in he said, 'I had an early one last night. Even the best of us need our rest.' I laughed and he drove off, just like that, but I know it was him up there.

"All the way home I was wondering why he lied, so later on this morning I made up my mind to go back and have a look around, then come on up to see you—but I lost track of the time, I guess. . . ."

He stopped talking and I heard a chair scrape—maybe he got up and gave her a kiss—but when he went on, his voice was softer, and I had to lean back against the door so that I could hear.

"There'd be nobody working on the culvert, being Sunday, so I took the detour, looking out for Ben's tire tracks where they might have hit the soft stuff. They were there too. I reckon it took no more than five minutes before I spotted them. I knew they were his because of the Michelin tread. That's the tires the cops use. So I followed him.

"He must have dropped down to the edge of the dam

about five hundred yards above the detour. There's been a landslide up there. Nothing big, but one side of the hill has come away, probably with all the spring rain. Ben would have gone around it, I guess, but he was in a four-wheel drive; I only had the Chevy, so I left it, and went on by foot. That's how come I found the fossils.

"I went over the top and there was a gully, running down toward the dam. That's where he'd gone. His tracks were there, plain as day. I followed them for about three hundred yards, then they went crazy, zigzagging everywhere . . . like he was chasing something . . . then they petered out in a clearing. I reckon he was chasing something. See? I reckon he was on to—"

As he spoke my father's car turned into the yard. I heard a scuffle behind me as I jumped up and guessed that Bobby was leaving through the front door.

My father stopped and looked down at the rocks on the newspaper. "What's this?" he said. "Mud pies?" Without waiting for me to answer, he stepped over them and went into the kitchen.

That night I was sitting up in bed reading *A Young Person's Guide to the Stone Ages* when Julia came in and sat beside me. She'd come from the bathroom and smelled delicious.

"What's that smell?" I said, breathing in.

"It's not called a *smell,* stupid; it's called a *fragrance.*"

I loved Julia when she put on airs. "Excuse me," I said. "What's the name of that fragrance?"

"It's called Sandalwood and it's from India."

"India? Pooh. No wonder it stinks. I read that you can't even swim in the Ganges because of all the turds."

As I hoped, she took the bait. "Kim, this particular

fragrance . . ." she paused to sniff the inside of her wrist, ". . . has been worn by women of influence for over four thousand years."

"So," I said, returning to my book, "where did you get it then?"

"From the catalog. Mom ordered it for me."

She meant the pharmaceutical catalog which was supplied to the office monthly. It was so highly valued that back issues, stained, spotted, and minus tear-out coupons, were stacked in our bathroom. Over the years, a thousand lingering references to this pile had taught me all there was to know about genitalia (both male and female and the causes and cures of the diseases thereof), warts (and their removal), laxatives (for the passage of either hard or soft stools) and the recommended medications for flatulence. That was how I knew without even needing to ask that Julia's Sandalwood had been ordered from this catalog, but I just wanted to hear her say so.

In the silence that followed I licked my finger noisily, turned a page and pretended to be engrossed in my research. This was an annoying trick that I had learned from Julia.

Eventually she leaned back and looked at me, resting her head on her hand. "I called Bobby tonight to see if he got home all right," she began. "I thought that you'd be glad to hear that he did."

Not knowing what direction this conversation might take, I said, "Oh," and turned a page. I sensed her stiffen.

"And," she continued, her voice simmering with threat, "unless you stop being so ignorant and give me your full attention, those lily white fingers will never turn another page."

I closed the book on my chest.

Assured that I was listening, she began again. "You might be interested to know that after we'd talked for a while, he said that he'd like to take you up the North Arm to collect some more of those fossils. Maybe even camp out for a night, if you're allowed."

I wasn't prepared for this. I gaped at her. "Well?" she said, shaking my arm. "Do you want to go or not?"

"Yes," I stammered, "but . . ."

"But what?"

"Would you come too?"

"I might," she said in a careless way.

I needed reassurance. "Julia, you didn't ask Bobby to take me, did you?"

She laughed. "Of course I didn't. He suggested it himself."

I considered this. "When do you think we'd be going?"

"Depends. Bobby says maybe after Christmas he can get time. Maybe New Year. He could make it like a holiday."

"Has he got camping things?"

"Sure. He's got all that."

"And food. Would he do the cooking?"

I had pushed too far.

"Yes, yes," she snapped. "He'd look after all that. What would you expect?"

During this conversation she had been flicking through the pages of my book, pausing here and there to examine the illustrations. When I said no more, she looked up. "You know," she said, "you're a bit like our father sometimes, aren't you? He's interested in weird creatures and that sort of stuff . . . which reminds me . . ." she closed the book and put it on my bedside table, ". . . why didn't you tell us that he'd come home this afternoon?"

"I didn't know," I answered truthfully. "The car appeared out of nowhere."

Her eyes narrowed. "How come? How come it did that? I know you. You can hear that car coming from the other side of the dam, can't you? But not this time, hey? And you were right there—right at the back door, weren't you?"

I dropped my eyes.

"I know what it was," she said, leaning closer. "You were too busy listening to Bobby and me, weren't you?"

My trembling bottom lip betrayed me.

"Well," she said, unrelenting, "did you learn anything?"

"A bit," I mumbled.

"A bit? What's a bit?"

"I heard how Bobby found the fossils."

"And? Go on . . ."

"And about Ben Cullen. How Bobby saw Ben Cullen . . ."

"Ben Cullen," she snapped. "What did you hear about Ben Cullen?"

I could never keep a thing from Julia. "How Bobby saw him without any lights. And how he was after something . . ."

She was very close, leaning right over me. "Something? What 'something'?"

"I don't know. Maybe an animal . . ."

She sat up. "What sort of animal? An elephant? A gorilla?"

"A pig? A feral pig?"

She knew that I was lying. Leaning close again, she whispered, "You listen to me. Whatever it was, he won't catch it. Not Ben. I guarantee."

Although I had great confidence in Julia, she wasn't always right.

nine

When December came my head was filled with plans for Christmas. I was especially excited about the idea of making everyone their own personalized present, instead of buying something boring from the Jericho Co-op like I usually did. But I never could keep a secret. I told Julia about my plan as we walked home from school the day before we broke up for the holidays. I didn't notice that she wasn't listening until I asked her what she would like and no answer came. She was lagging behind, her shoes in her hand, kicking up dust with her bare feet.

"Hey," I said, "you're not even listening."

She made a face. "I *was* listening. But I don't see why I should look forward to Christmas."

How could she not look forward to Christmas? The idea was ridiculous. Every year, usually in August, my mother went down to the city shops to choose our presents at the sales. She would put everything away and then, just before the Big Day, a van would arrive, special delivery, and parcels would disappear into the cellar, where we were least likely to go.

My mother always bought the right thing for Christmas. The year that I wanted a stamp album, I got the best, plus a collection of stamps and a backlit magnifying glass to go with it. The year that I wanted a set of encyclopedia, that's what I got. It was the same for

Julia—records, clothes, exactly what she wanted. So when she said, "I don't see why I should look forward to Christmas," I thought that she had a touch of the December sun.

"You're just being stupid," I said, and walked off. I didn't get far. She grabbed my schoolbag and hauled me around to face her.

"What?" I said, bracing myself for a teeth rattler, but she wasn't angry; she looked as if she was going to cry.

"You don't know what you're talking about," she said.

"I was talking about Christmas. And you said—"

She waved her hands in my face to shut me up. "I know that. What I meant was, what happens *after* Christmas. That's what's wrong. Not Christmas. And you're the one who's stupid."

After Christmas there was still four weeks holiday. I gave her a blank look. She sighed. "At the end of January I get packed off to boarding school. Remember?"

Then I understood. "Sorry, Jules," I said, and we walked the rest of the way home in silence.

I had already finished one of the presents. In the bottom drawer of my wardrobe, beneath my winter clothes stored in camphor, was something special that I had made at school.

It was routine that every Friday afternoon all the students attended craft classes. The girls went to sewing, where they worked on embroidering a sampler copied from a design specified by the teacher, Miss Dawson. One year Miss Dawson instructed the girls to chain-stitch the words "A Woman's Work Is Never Done" in the center of their samplers. Julia begged to be able to take hers home and, thinking that she had found a zealous student, Miss Dawson agreed. The next Friday, when the girls laid out their work on the lids of their sewing baskets ready for inspection, Miss Dawson's eyes were opened. In the center of Julia's sampler was a love heart, pierced by an arrow, with "Bobby for Julia" cross-stitched inside. The letters *JM* and *BO'M* appeared over and over around the border. Miss Dawson declared that this work "lacked taste" and dismissed Julia from the class. Julia was delighted.

The boys did leatherwork with Mr. D'Arcy. From Monday morning to Friday lunch he was a monster; from Friday lunch to three o'clock go-home-time he was a human being. Better, he was an artist. Out of his back pocket he produced a leather wallet that he had made himself. It showed the head of a dog; a retriever, he said, although every boy could see exactly what it was without being told. But when he said, "That's taken from life. That's my dog Jessie," he had the class in the palm of his hand. For one and a half hours every Friday, D'Arcy was a boy's best friend; he taught every one of us how to make something wonderful: What he called a "presentation bookmark." Each boy was given a piece of leather which he trimmed to a specified size and cut into thin strips at one end, like a feathery tail. When this was finished, he approached D'Arcy for advice on the design to be tooled into it.

When my turn came I couldn't make up my mind. Most boys had chosen leaves or four-leafed clovers because they were easy.

D'Arcy called me by name. He said, "Well, Kim, what's it to be for you?"

"I don't know, Sir," I admitted. "I'd like to do a bat. But

I'd like an eagle too." I expected that he would laugh.

"A bat," he repeated, "or an eagle." He gave me a strange look. "So, we have a flyer, have we?" And before I had time to reply, he took a sharp pencil from behind his ear and outlined the head of an eagle on my strip of leather. "Right," he said. "Now you work that up properly. You've got a nice gift in the making there."

That was how D'Arcy got me started on making everyone a present for Christmas. I finished the eagle-headed bookmark and put it away for my father. I could have given it to my mother to use in her accounts book, but I had something different in mind for her.

In the history section at the library was a framed brass rubbing from a tomb in Westminster Abbey. When I asked about it, Miss Dunne produced a book that described how rubbings were made. That was where I got the idea for my mother's present. I suggested to Miss Dunne that the shell fossils Bobby had found might be able to be rubbed in the same way. She agreed. She said that when she was a girl if the sermon in church was too long her father would give her the collection coins to mind. She'd rub them with the stub of a pencil on the cigarette papers that he kept in his pocket. He called these drawings "poor man's money" and dared her to put them in the plate, but she never did. Miss Dunne warned me that the paper I chose would have to be just right: Not so thin that it tore, but not so thick that the shape of the fossil wouldn't show through—and I would have to use the right crayon: Not too soft or it would crumble; not too hard or it would scratch.

In spite of all these difficulties, I decided that I would make a set of fossil shell rubbings for my mother.

When Pa Cossey came in next, I waited until he'd fin-ished talking to my father, then I followed him out into the yard. He thought that I was waiting for the surprise he usually brought.

"Sorry, Kimmy," he said, "but I haven't got anything for you today. Didn't even know that I was coming until this morning, when I woke up with my back out. Next time . . ."

"No, Pa," I said, "I only wanted to ask you something."

He was happier then and we sat on the kitchen step to have a talk. First I told him about my plans to make the presents, then about the bookmark, then about Miss Dunne and the fossil rubbings. "If I can do four little rub-bings, all the same size, like a set," I said, "I wondered if you could give me some ideas on how to make frames for them. I want Mom to hang them in the reception room."

"Frames?" he said. "Out of wood?"

I nodded.

"What size?"

I showed him, forming a square with my thumbs and fingers. "Not big," I said.

"How many did you say?"

"Four. All the same size, but all the rubbings would be of different shells. A matching set, like the ones you see in interior decorating magazines."

"For your mother, eh? For Christmas?" He was pulling at the lobe of his ear, thinking.

I waited.

Finally he clapped his hands on his knees and stood up. "Well," he said, pressing his hands into the small of his back, "since it so happens that I like your mom, and since it seems that you like her too, how about this: If you get those drawings to me, say, a week before Christmas, I reckon that I can do something for you. How about that?"

I said that would be very good and more than I had hoped for. The drawings would be on time. I wouldn't let him down. "You won't be disappointed," I said. "I promise."

I reached out to shake his hand, like always, but he did something that he'd never done before. He grabbed me around the shoulders and hugged me. He held me so hard that I felt his heart beat, then he let me go and headed out the back gate. My own father never hugged me like that.

In spite of my promise to Pa, progress on the rubbings was not good. Everything Miss Dunne warned me about happened. I had to make do with whatever materials I could find at Frank Tassel's News and Casket: Kids' stuff, sealed up in cardboard packets with yellow suns and blue skies and green trees shaped like toffee apples printed all over them. I told Frank what I was after. He thought about it. He knew that my parents would pay. After a minute he disappeared into the back of his shcp. When he came out he pushed a book at me. "Here," he said, "have a look in this. Take it home if you want. Nobody's ever used it before, but if you find what you're after, I can phone in an order and get it delivered with next week's magazines."

The book was an art supplies catalog, the first of many that I would come to own.

My order arrived the same afternoon I had fallen out with Julia about Christmas. I came home to find a brown-paper parcel with my name on it sitting on the kitchen table. "Frank Tassel dropped that in himself," my mother said. "He assured me that you ordered it, so I paid him . . ."

She was waiting for me to explain. "Thanks," I said, picking it up, "but I can't tell you what it is. You have to trust me. It's a secret for Christmas."

She let me go, but as I reached the door I heard Julia mutter, "Every day is Christmas Day for Mommy's darling pet. . . ."

I went straight to my room and opened the parcel. Inside was exactly what I had ordered: Art paper, not too rough and not too smooth, not too thick and not too thin; and a packet of twelve crayons: Four brown, four black, four white, each wrapped in its own paper jacket and marked "Artist Quality."

After dinner I started work and by nine o'clock I was satisfied that I could make something worthwhile for my mother. I put all the materials away in my desk and went downstairs to say good-night. Julia's door was shut so I left her alone. I fell asleep happy.

Much later the sound of car doors slamming woke me. I sat up. Julia was standing at my window looking down into the yard.

"What is it?" I asked, but she ignored me and I got up to see for myself.

Three vehicles were parked in our yard. Our car was there, and the Fergusons' pickup. Lights were flashing everywhere and people moved among them, but no one I recognized—until I saw the sergeant and another man supporting a yellow-haired girl between them. I guessed what had happened.

"They've caught one," I whispered. "Haven't they?"

Julia let the curtain fall. "They get all of us sooner or later," she said, and vanished into the hall.

I lifted the curtain and looked back into the yard. The lights were gone and it was dark and quiet, but as I watched I saw a pinpoint of light in the shadow beneath my window. Someone was smoking a cigarette. I pressed my face against the glass and made out a figure in uniform. It was Ben Cullen, standing alone.

I pulled on my dressing gown, intending to go down, but just as I reached my bedroom door I heard footsteps on the stairs and there was my mother, and right behind her Keithy Ferguson, wearing blue-and-white-striped pajamas and grinning from ear to ear. "Hey, Kim," he said, very chirpy.

Keithy Ferguson was a country kid through and through. He never even came to town when his mother picked up the family's groceries from the co-op on Saturday mornings; it was no wonder I stood gaping at him standing outside my bedroom door in the middle of the night.

My mother ushered us both into my room. "Listen," she said, sitting me down on the end of my bed. "Keith's parents have had some trouble and had to come in. They couldn't leave him out there alone. I want you to look after him until we sort things out downstairs. You can get him a drink or something from the kitchen, but I don't want you around the office. Do you understand?" She spoke directly into my face, all the while holding my chin to prevent me from watching Keithy, who loitered dangerously close to my desk. "Do you understand?" she repeated. I nodded.

Satisfied, she released me and turned her attention to him. "Keith," she said, using a voice that she reserved for kids who misbehaved in the office, "I'm sure that you've got quite a story to tell, but we don't want rumors starting, so . . ." she trailed off, waving a warning finger as she left the room.

Keithy's eyes returned to my desk. I acted fast to protect my things. "Well," I said, "would you like a drink? I could make you a hot chocolate."

"No thanks," he said. "If I end up sleeping here, I might wet the bed." He said this so matter-of-factly that I was taken by surprise. "Lots of kids do, you know, and even grown-ups. I never have a drink before bed. But I wouldn't mind a biscuit. Or some cake."

"We've got cake," I said, but as I slipped off the bed, motioning for him to follow, I saw his expression change. I looked behind me. Julia stood in the doorway.

"Hmm, cake . . ." she began, her voice smooth as honey. "Could a girl join this party, or is it just a midnight snack for the men?"

Keithy's eyes were round as saucers. Julia in a nightie, her hair spilling over her shoulders, was a sight to see.

"Keith might have to spend the night," I said. "His mom and dad have come in . . ."

". . . with that Flannagan girl," she concluded, slipping past me to drop onto my bed. "So, Keithy, are you going to tell us what happened, or are you going to eat cake and run?"

She was being unfair and she knew it. Keith looked from her to me. As a guest he was obliged to answer her, but since she was obviously baiting him, he would have preferred to escape with me. I suggested a compromise:

Keith and I could get cake from the kitchen, if Julia could wait for the story of the night's events.

"Good idea," she yawned, lying back, her hands behind her head. "And while you're down there, Kimmy, I've got no objection to a hot chocolate myself."

In the kitchen I had time to settle Keithy down. "She's just showing off," I told him. "You know, because she doesn't know you."

He wasn't convinced, I could tell.

When the chocolate was made and the cake sliced, I put everything onto a tray and went back to the bedroom, with Keithy following. When we were settled Julia said, "Well Keithy, are you going to tell us or do I have to drag it out of you?"

He wiped some cake crumbs from his mouth and looked at her long and hard. "You know, my mother says that you've got a bad reputation—but I don't care. I reckon that you're the best looking girl I've ever seen."

Keithy Ferguson got the better of Julia that night. She blushed scarlet, took a sip of her chocolate, then said very seriously, "Thanks, Keithy. I accept the compliment, and I reckon you look pretty good yourself . . . especially in those pajamas."

This marked a truce. I winked at Keithy, who took the hint. "So," he said, "if you want me to tell you what happened, you better get comfortable, because it's a pretty long story. Okay?"

Julia put her chocolate on my bedside table, fluffed up my pillows and settled in. I leaned back against her legs. If she minded, she didn't say.

Keithy had gone to bed as usual but was woken by a commotion in the chicken yard. He got up straight away, only to bump into his father, who was reaching for his gun in the hall. "It might be a fox," he said, "or it might be them kids," and they went into the yard together. The chicken yard was behind their shed, and they waited at the corner to take a look before they barged in.

"Sure enough," Keithy said, "there they were. The moon wasn't full, but we could see them clear enough. The girl was taller, with yellow hair, and the other one, well . . . you saw on the road after the Spring Dance."

"Was it a boy?" Julia interrupted.

Keithy nodded. "I'd say it was a boy. About as old as us, maybe. But it was the girl we could really see. She looked like she had something in her dress, that she was carrying something in a fold of her dress. Eggs, we reckoned, since we found them later, all smashed where they were dropped. My father yelled, 'Hey! You two . . .' and the little one, he took off. She tried to go, but her dress got caught on the wire gate and she started calling out. Not in English, I don't reckon. In the car coming here, I told that to the sergeant. I said I couldn't understand what she said, and I didn't think it was English. The sergeant said that I might be right. Anyway, whatever she was saying, the boy got away, but when he saw she wasn't behind him, he came back. That's when my father had enough. He fired one shot straight up, just one shot, and the boy took off again, heading for the bush, but she went crazy. When she heard that shot, she pulled herself free—except she ran the wrong way. She ran straight back into the henhouse and trapped herself. That's what she did. Trapped herself."

He reached out to take some cake and ate it while we waited. When he was ready, he went on.

"My dad walked up to the gate and I followed him. The henhouse is a shed about as big as this room. There's rows of laying boxes in there, see. There's no way out. There's a window right up near the roof, but she would never get out of that. We went up to the door and looked in. It was black as pitch in there. Then my mother came out. She'd heard the shot, that's what got her going. My father told her what happened and she went for him because he used the gun. 'The poor kid will be scared to death,' she said. She told us to get right out of the way, and when we did she went in, talking gentle like you do to a sick animal, see; she was saying, 'It's all right, dear. It's all right, dear,' over and over.

"After a while she came back to the door. 'You can call the sergeant,' she said. 'And get the doctor too.' Then she went back. I don't know what she was doing, but she was still there when Ben Cullen came . . . "

"Ben Cullen," Julia said, sitting up. "I thought you called the sergeant."

"We did. We called the station, but it was the sergeant's night off and Ben came instead. He drove right into the yard with all his lights blazing like a big show-off, and he walked straight into the henhouse, smart as you like, with his giant flashlight shining everywhere. I was outside, but I heard what happened. There was screaming, something terrible, then my mother yelling, 'Get out! Get out of here!' Next thing Ben comes back holding his hand up to his face. He was bleeding. All down his cheek was scratched. My mom said that he grabbed the girl and tried to pull her out, see. She was under the laying boxes and he tried to grab her. Well, he got what was coming to him. Then your dad came. First he took a look at Ben, then he went into the henhouse with Mom. Ben stood aside. He kept right out of it, but my dad, he went back to the house and rang the sergeant at home. He only lives ten minutes away, up near the Andersons'. Anyway, nothing happened then, not for a while, until the doc came out and the girl was between him and my mom, sagging sort of, and they were propping her up. They won't tell how they did it, but I reckon the doc got a needle into her; some drug, I bet . . ."

"He wouldn't hurt her," I interrupted.

"No, I'm not saying he would. Hey, your dad, he brought me into the world. He's always been nice to me. But I'm saying he must have done something a bit different, because they won't tell me, see, and I saw how she looked when she came out; all dopey. So, anyway, that's how they got her into your car, into the back, and then the serge came, and after that there was a big confab. The serge went over to Ben and gave him a serve. He called him for everything, told him he was irresponsible, a disgrace to the force. I heard it all. Boy, did he cop it. Then we came in here. My mom went with the girl in your dad's car and my dad came in too, in the pickup, but the serge said I could go with him in the Landrover. I saw Ben coming behind us but he didn't come into your house; the serge told him to stay in the yard with the cars—to listen for calls. He was still the officer on duty, see? And that's the whole story. Not bad, hey?"

I thought it was an excellent story but I wasn't satisfied; the best part had been left out as far as I was concerned. "So," I said, "what does she look like? Is she creepy?"

Keithy didn't understand. "I told you what she looked like. She was bigger than him and she had this long yellow hair."

I tried again. "I mean her face and all that. Was she ugly? With rotten teeth and—"

"You're disgusting," Julia said, thumping me in the middle of the back. "She's a human being, not the creature from the black lagoon."

Keithy answered me anyway. "I never saw her properly, not close up. My father pulled me away when they brought her out. All I saw was her between my mom and your dad. She had long yellow hair out like this . . ." he held his hands out from his shoulders, ". . . that's all I saw. And a dress on. A baggy-looking thing. I saw that." He put his tongue out and licked cake crumbs from around his mouth.

Julia pushed me away and leaned forward. "Keithy," she said, "you know when Ben went in after her, do you think she would have seen him? His face, I mean?"

"She might. He had an awful big flashlight." He held his hands apart to indicate the size.

"No. I mean, would she have known that it was him. That it was Ben himself?"

"Jules," I said, "how would she know Ben Cullen? She's been living way out in the bush."

"So, Mr. Know-all, why didn't she scratch Keithy's mother too? And our father?"

I shook my head. Sometimes Julia didn't think straight. "Because she went in quietly," I said, "and Ben came in like an idiot . . ."

"And he might have grabbed her," Keithy added, suddenly understanding the possibilities of what he hadn't seen. "He might have even grabbed her by the hair. It's longer than yours, and sticks out wild everywhere. That's what happened, I bet."

Julia got up and went to the window. "Anyway, his car's gone now," she said. She turned to Keithy and patted him on the shoulder. "Your parents might be here for a while. They'll be waiting to see if the girl's all right. Maybe you'd better lie down with Kim and go to sleep. It's late, and tomorrow's the last day of school, remember."

When she'd gone, I turned out the light and pulled back the covers of my bed. Keithy and I stretched out side by side on the sheets. He said that there were some things he couldn't tell when Julia was there; things that would frighten girls. But he could tell me, now that we were alone.

"What things?" I prodded. He didn't answer me straight off and I waited while he considered. The moonlight through the lace dappled his skin cream and gray.

First, he said, she had a terrible smell. A smell like a stinking wet dog. When she went past him with my father, he smelled her. And there were scabs. He saw them too. Big scabs on the palms of her hands and on her knees. Or calluses. He wasn't exactly sure, but they would be from running like a dog. When she got free of the gate and ran into the henhouse, she fell down on all fours like a dog. That was how she dropped the eggs. Another thing was her eyes. When he stood in the door-way of the henhouse with his father, and said that it was pitch black inside; well it was, except for two yellow eyes that stared back. These eyes didn't blink. They narrowed into slits. Also, he could explain the scratches on Ben

Cullen's face. This was because of her fingernails. Ben told him about the nails while he was waiting for the sergeant. They were yellow, and curled under like claws.

And what about the other one, I asked, had he seen him too?

Only from a distance, he said. Not as close as he'd seen the girl. But close enough. He'd seen him run. Not on the ground like the girl, but bent low, with his shoulders forward, his arms hanging loose and his head turning from side to side. Looking. Listening. Scenting. Then he disappeared into the shadows, into the dark bush.

Keithy was gone when I woke up. He might not have been there at all except for a wet patch the size of a dinner plate on the sheet beside me.

There was no one in the kitchen, no signs of breakfast, though the sink and the kitchen table were covered in unwashed cups. I looked out the back door. All the cars were gone except for ours. I went upstairs to Julia's room. She was already dressed for school and making her bed. "Where is everybody?" I said.

She shook her head. "Still with the girl, I suppose. You'd better get going if you don't want to be late." I turned to leave, but she called, "Is Keithy still here?"

"No," I said, "but he left a little message in my bed."

"What sort of message?"

"He piddled in it."

She laughed. "Well, you'll have to clean it up yourself. Mom won't be making your bed this morning, that's for sure."

I got ready for school and did what I could with my bed. Julia didn't help; she was on the phone to Bobby.

When it was time to leave we went into the office. Nobody was there, not in the reception room nor in the examining room, but the door of the single overnight room was ajar. Julia knocked and waited as we had been taught. I stood behind her. There was a movement inside, then my mother opened the door a bit more. She was still in her dressing gown, her face was pale, and she looked sick. She tried to smile. "Is it that time already?" she said. She stood right in the doorway, holding the door.

"It's the last day of school," I said, stepping forward. She didn't hear me. She was looking back into the room when I spoke. I caught sight of my father behind her, bending over the bed. My mother pulled the door closed even further.

"We're off," Julia said, and my mother nodded.

"It's not much fun here," she whispered. "Not much fun at all. I'll see you tonight."

This was a rotten start to the last day of school, and it got worse. Keithy Ferguson didn't show up, so when everyone arrived I told his story for him. I told them about the wild girl running like a dog, and the calluses and the claws and her brother loping off into the bush. Thomas Watts, the crybaby of the third grade, went teary eyed and snivelled, but I wasn't sure that the rest believed me. They listened and their mouths were open, but afterward they nudged each other.

Julia took no part in this. She seemed to change as soon as she walked through the school gates. The other girls were crying because Darling McMurtry was going to a hairdressing school out of state. Julia ignored them. She even ignored the O'Meara boys, Bobby's cousins, who were expecting her to have some fun, especially since this was her last day ever at the Jericho school.

I saw her again at morning recess, prowling about all alone, looking into classrooms and hanging around in doorways. I said, "What's the matter with you, Jules?"

She shrugged and tried to get away but I stood in front of her and blocked her escape.

She said, "I'm just taking a last look, that's all."

I thought she was joking. "A last look? I thought that you could hardly wait to leave."

"I had some fun here," she said, then pushed me out of the way.

After lunch, when all the drinks were gone and the watermelon eaten, the teachers said that we could go home. Bobby turned up at the gate just as we were leaving. I guessed that this was prearranged.

"What about a drive up to Bella Vista?" he said. I knew that he wasn't talking to me so I let them go and walked home alone.

When I turned into our backyard I saw a few cars parked in the drive outside the office and knew that my parents must be busy. I went in by the kitchen door and dropped my schoolbag on the floor. The unwashed cups from the night before were still piled everywhere. I had poured a glass of water and sat down at the table, all ready to feel sorry for myself, when my mother came in. Her white uniform was grubby. She looked even worse than she had that morning. Her eyes were dark and her hair was untidy. "I thought I heard someone come in," she said. "You're early."

"It's the last day of school, remember?" I used an *I've-already-told-you-that* tone.

"I know. Mrs. Watts reminded me." Her voice was

sharp; she stood behind a chair. She looked at me as if she had said something significant.

"Big fat Mrs. Watts," I joked, not understanding.

She didn't laugh. She leaned forward, putting her weight on the back of the chair. "No. Not big fat Mrs. Watts; just ordinary Mrs. Watts whose son Thomas came home from school in tears after someone told a story that frightened the life out of him."

Now I understood. I saw the flabby, watery face of Thomas Watts in the front row of my story-time spectacular. I dropped my eyes to the rim of my glass.

"Is it true? Did you tell everyone about last night?"

I nodded, feeling tears forming.

"And did you add a load of rubbish about fangs and claws and children running like dogs?"

"I never said anything about fangs," I muttered.

"Kim," she said, "why did you do it? I specifically warned you about the danger of rumors. But what you have done is worse. Much worse. Claws, for heaven's sake. Where on earth did all this nonsense come from?"

I thought about blaming Keithy. I hadn't invented it all myself—I heard it from him first. But I knew that it wasn't his fault, any more than it was the fault of the darkness, or the drifting lace of the curtains, or the moonlight spilling across my bed.

"I'm sorry," I said, feeling the tears start to roll. "I was stupid. Just stupid. Like Julia always says."

Her expression didn't soften. "No," she said, "more cruel than stupid. Cruel and irresponsible. Cruel because you were talking about other people's lives and injuring them. Irresponsible because I distinctly told you not to talk about it." She sat down and reached across the table to hold my hand. I cried even harder. I wouldn't have hurt my mother for anything.

"Kimmy," she began again, "that girl hasn't got claws or fangs. She's got some pretty terrible cuts and bruises, but they're not from running like a dog . . . is that what you told them, really? That she ran like a dog?"

"Yes," I blubbered.

She took her hands away and sat back, looking at me. "I haven't told your father, and I don't think I will. He might not be as lenient as me. You know his temper. But I know this town too—and I'm telling you that there will be trouble coming from this. . . ."

"What sort of trouble?" I asked, my voice breaking.

She got up from the table before she answered. "Rumors. Gossip. Maybe worse."

I looked at her, uncomprehending.

"Look, maybe this is partly our fault. Maybe we should have told you more before you went to school, but we just didn't have the chance. What I'm trying to tell you is that we've got one very unhappy girl in there. She's filthy, she's half-starved, she's frightened. On top of that she sprained her ankle trying to get away from that lout Cullen, so she can hardly walk—and now you've as good as offered an open invitation for the whole town to come and take a look—as if she's the main attraction at a sideshow."

I started crying and she put her arm around my shoulder. "Poor Kimmy," was all she said, but she patted me and stroked my head.

When I had settled to sobbing and sniffing, she stopped patting and said, "Where was your sister when all this was going on? Did she hear?"

I told her about Julia's last day; how she had wandered around the school, and that Bobby had picked her up later. I felt her hands on my shoulders. "Yes," she sighed. "There's another one with troubles." Then she seemed to recover. "Look, you know that your father and I are busy with the girl, and I don't think that Julia's going to be in any mood to entertain you when she gets back. The best thing that you can do is keep out of everybody's way; find something quiet to do, and wait till this mess blows over. Hopefully, for everybody's sake, before Christmas." She gave me a few solid pats on the back. "There. Consider yourself punished."

I was glad to get off so lightly—and I took her reference to Christmas as a good sign. Until she said that, there was a possibility that the Big Day might miss me altogether.

I went up to my room and dropped onto my bed. It was hot, I was very tired, and in no time I drifted off into a deep sleep.

Julia woke me up, shaking me, and calling my name. "Kim," she was saying, directly into my face, "Kim. What's going on? Kim . . ."

I sat up, feeling dull and groggy. "What?" I said. "What's wrong?"

"I've just come back from Queenie's and everybody's saying . . . " She sat on the side of the bed and repeated the whole terrible story. This time the source of the information wasn't snivelling Thomas Watts, or his blabbermouth mother, but the older brothers and sisters of the kids at school, and their mothers, fathers, aunts, uncles and any other family hangers-on . . . according to Julia. She went on and on: The claws, the fangs, the scabs; and already a few new twists and turns had been added to liven up the story. The girl had bitten Ben Cullen and he might have to get a rabies shot; the boy's upper teeth protruded over his bottom lip like a vampire's. . . . I couldn't listen. I turned away from her before she'd finished.

But Julia was not my mother. She reached across the bed and shook me until my teeth snapped together. "Are you crazy?" she hissed. "Are you absolutely mad?"

I could stand anything but Julia hating me—anything—but I didn't cry because that would only make things worse. I set my face hard. "Does everybody know that it was me?" I asked.

She stopped shaking me when I spoke. "Ben Cullen's got a big mouth too," she said.

I rolled over. Her face was directly above mine. She breathed with her mouth open. Her teeth glinted white against her lips. Her eyes were narrow slits; her black hair fell across her face and twisted around her neck.

I waited, terrified.

She saw my fear and sat back, pushing her hair from her face. "You're lucky," she said. "He's a bigger idiot than you. He's been down at the pub shooting his stupid mouth off all afternoon. So you're lucky. You're covered."

Sensing that the worst was over, I said, "Did anyone think that it was Keith?"

"Keith? Nobody mentioned Keith. Why would anybody think it was him?"

I felt better. I sat up against the pillows and rubbed my face and eyes. She watched me the whole time, then she said, "Did you see in the backyard?"

I shook my head. I had no idea what might be in the yard.

"There's at least six cars. The office is full of people. Snooping, I bet. All hoping for a look. It's you who did that and I hope you're satisfied."

I slipped off the bed and looked down. It was nearly dark, but I could see the dim shapes of cars in the yard.

I looked back. "I already talked to Mom," I said. "And she went for me too. I was stupid . . ."

"Very stupid. The stupidest ever."

". . . But I said I was sorry, so . . ."

I lost my willpower then. I lost all pride and determination. I just couldn't get along without her liking me. I started to cry. I tried to pretend that I wasn't, turning back to the window, but she could tell what was happening by the way I was shaking. My shoulders were shaking so much that even when I grabbed the window sill I couldn't stop.

She got up and came to stand behind me. She didn't touch me; she was too angry for that. She said, "Well, I hope that you've learned a lesson. Now come on. There's no point in blubbering. Come downstairs and I'll make you some toast. That's the best offer you're going to get around this place for a while."

Cars came and went. The phone rang constantly. I went to bed without a single good-night.

ten

as soon as I woke up the next morning, I thought of the girl downstairs. All night I'd heard voices and sometimes what I thought was crying.

When I went down to the kitchen my mother was already there, standing at the back door with her coffee, looking out into the yard.

"You're ready early," I said. She was in her uniform although it was another hour before the office usually opened.

"I'm expecting the sergeant," she said. "He's coming to set up a time for the welfare people to visit Colleen—and there's bound to be a few busybodies soon." She sipped her coffee and sighed. "It's going to be another big day."

Julia came in and heard part of this. "Colleen?" she said. "Is that her name?"

My mother looked back from the doorway. "So her uncle told the sergeant."

Julia sat at the table and helped herself to toast. "I never thought of her having a proper name," she said. "I always thought her father would call her 'Hey, you!' like a dog."

"Her father's dead," my mother reminded her.

Julia was unrepentant. "Good," she muttered, under her breath.

"I thought I heard crying last night," I said, hinting that I wanted to know more.

I was ignored. I guessed that my storytelling episode was the reason. Julia must have reached the same conclusion. "Come on," she said, "I'm sure Kim's learned his lesson. And you have to tell us sometime."

My mother took a sip of her coffee. She was thinking about this. Finally, she said, "I suppose so, provided it doesn't leave this house. Not like last time." She stared hard at me. "Up until last night your father kept her sedated so we could get her cleaned up. She's been bathed and dressed and I trimmed her nails. Then about midnight she started to come around. She was bright enough to work out that she was locked in—and she wasn't going to have any of that—so she tried to get away. But with her ankle, she couldn't do much about it . . . that's what started the crying you would have heard."

"What's wrong with her ankle?" Julia said.

"Ben Cullen did it," I started in—but one look shut me up.

"It's sprained. We think it happened when Ben tried to grab hold of her at the Fergusons'."

"Typical," Julia sneered.

"Apart from that, she drank some tea and I got her to use the toilet. A major achievement after a few accidents . . ."

Julia stopped eating. "Charming," she said.

My mother left the doorway and put her cup on the table. She was laughing at Julia. "You'd never make a nurse, would you? Anyway, that's the story so far—except that when I left her ten minutes ago she was sitting on the floor wrapped up in a blanket. And your father's just gone to bed."

I suspected there was much more to tell. "Did she say anything?" I asked. "Keithy said that he heard her talk, but not in English. He said—"

She covered her ears. "No more Keithy stories. He told you a lot of things, I'm sure; but believe me, he was wrong there. She might not use the Queen's English, but she can talk, I assure you."

"And is she pretty?" Julia asked. "We never got to see her properly, Kimmy and me, but Ruby Parsons told Bobby that she was pretty."

"As far as I know, Ruby saw her once—and once only—sitting in her father's pickup. On the basis of that, half of Jericho thinks that we've got Cinderella in there; the other half thinks she's a monster—depending on what story they heard." She looked at me again. "Once and for all, Colleen's an ordinary girl who's had an awful life, that's what I think. Right now she looks terrible, it's true. She's badly undernourished. She's covered in scratches and bites." She shook her head in despair. "That should do for starters. All I know is that it's up to us to get her settled . . ."

Julia didn't let her finish. "Up to us? I thought those welfare people were taking her?"

My mother smiled. "Welfare is always tied up in bureaucracy. Even if they come there's bound to be a thousand forms to fill in. Sorry, Jules, but I'm afraid we've got her for a while."

"What about her mother?"

"You know the answer to that."

Julia was persistent. "Her uncle then. He's the next of kin."

My mother was losing patience. She put her hands flat

on the table and leaned forward. "Julia, you're talking about a man who didn't even come to his own brother's inquest. Or his funeral. Use some common sense. Does he sound like the type who would accept responsibility for a girl like Colleen?"

Julia was cornered. "Well, it doesn't make her ours. She can't just come into someone's house and take—"

"Julia!" I jumped and Julia sat back, surprised. My mother glared at her. "How can you talk like that? What has anyone asked you to do? Have you had to bathe her? Or clean up her business? Or drag her filthy clothes off her while she called you every name under the sun? Have you? Answer me."

Julia looked down.

"No, you haven't. So don't you tell me who will—or won't—take responsibility for her. You don't know the half of it, do you hear?" She went back to the door and checked the yard. Satisfied that no car had come in, she returned to the table.

"Now listen to me, both of you. I was going to wait until your father woke up, so we could talk to you to-gether, but in the circumstances I'd better tell you now. Apart from the busybodies we're getting, somebody else might have a reason for wanting to see this girl. . . ." She looked from Julia to me. "She could be a murder witness, couldn't she? Did either of you think of that?"

I felt my stomach turn with fear; but not Julia. "Another reason why she shouldn't be here," she said, partly to herself.

My mother heard her. "Don't you think we know that? Don't you think we know the risks, all to protect a child who means nothing to us? Who literally came out of the trees? But that's what we have to do, isn't it . . . because it's the right thing. Good job we've got walls and bars, isn't it?"

Neither of us answered.

"But," my mother went on, "there's the little brother. He's still out there . . ." She pointed suddenly toward the door. "If we can get her settled—if we can build some trust—there's a chance we might learn where he is. Do you understand? Before he dies of starvation. Or some trigger-happy idiot gets to him with a gun. Not quite as simple now, is it, Miss Julia? Not quite so black and white?"

Julia squashed crumbs beneath her fingers.

"So, since Colleen should really go—as you point out—and since she should also stay, we've had to compromise. That's why the sergeant's coming this morning; not just to line up a visit from the welfare people—he could have done that over the phone. He's bringing in a police van from down the coast and we're going to put on a bit of a show. We're waiting until we get a few gossipy onlookers, then we're carrying out a stretcher. An empty stretcher, just to let everyone think that Colleen's gone. Do you understand? She'll still be here, safe and sound, but to the rest of Jericho she's gone."

Nothing like this had happened in The Laurels since Loony Pilcher stabbed the superintendent. I was amazed. Speechless.

"Who'll know the truth?" Julia asked.

"The four of us, the sergeant, the van drivers and one or two people from police headquarters. Nobody else."

"What about Ben Cullen?" Julia asked. "He's a cop."

My mother smiled. "He's also a big mouth. And incompetent. The sergeant isn't telling him."

Julia's voice softened. "Can I tell Bobby?"

"No."

"Will we have police staying here?" I asked. "For protection?"

"It's not that bad. The sergeant will always be around and he's not hard to contact. Otherwise, it's business as usual. Except there won't be any patients allowed near the overnight rooms. All right?"

It certainly wasn't all right. I was about to protest but my mother saw, and silenced me with a wave of her hand. "No more," she said. "I've probably told you too much already. I'm going to check on Colleen. Kim, keep an eye out for the sergeant. Julia, since you're always looking for something to manage, try thinking about this house for a couple of days. And both of you can get stuck into cleaning up this kitchen. Some of those cups have been sitting on the sink since last Thursday." As she left, she called from the hallway. "I love you both, you know that."

Julia was in a bad mood. We cleaned up the kitchen in silence and as soon as the dishes were finished, she headed for the door.

"Hey," I called, "where are you going?"

"Out," she said.

I put all the dishes away and tidied up, then went up to my room. At about ten I heard the police van drive in, and watched the pantomime of the empty stretcher from my window. At least three patients saw it too—from a distance prescribed by my mother and the sergeant. I spent the afternoon working on my fossil rubbings.

Julia reappeared just before dinner.

"Have you been with Bobby?" I said.

"You'll find out," she answered.

"Well, don't say you've been at Queenie's. Nobody could stay at Queenie's all day."

"You're right," she said, giving me one of her superior smiles. "Nobody could stay at Queenie's all day."

The next morning, which was Sunday, I did a few jobs for my mother, then went back to my room. At about nine o'clock, as I was happily lost in my rubbings, I heard somebody behind me and looked around. There was Julia, dressed in one of my mother's uniforms. She did a quick pirouette. "What do you think?" she asked.

I stared. "What are you doing with that on?" I said.

"Can I trust you to keep a secret?" she said, checking the hem in my mirror.

I snorted to show my contempt.

She perched on the edge of my bed and beckoned to me. I would have liked to refuse, but I couldn't. Julia's secrets were always the best. I put my things away in my desk and sat next to her.

"Yesterday," she said, using her lowest, most conspiratorial voice, "Bobby dropped into the pub at the Empire and Ruby came out and talked to me. She'd heard that the girl was gone and wanted to know if it was true, and all that. . . ."

"Did you say that it was?"

"Of course. We were as good as told to lie, weren't we? Anyway, then she asked me if I was doing anything before I left for boarding school. I told her that I was only hanging around here, so she asked me if I'd like a job waitressing. You know, with Christmas coming, and all the extra business. I said that I would, and she asked me to come down for a trial—today. So I'm doing four hours: From ten to two this afternoon. The lunch rush, Ruby called it. She said to wear a neat white dress . . . so . . ."

"But that's one of Mom's uniforms," I protested.

"Because I don't own a white dress, stupid. Have you ever seen me in a white dress?"

I never had, and changed the subject. "How much are you getting paid?" I asked.

"That's between Ruby and me," she said. She must have known I thought she was lying and added very quickly, "Maybe just enough to buy some mommy's boy a Christmas present, if he's lucky."

I considered this a reasonable answer, but it was part of the game to set up obstacles. "They'll murder you when they find out."

"Then don't tell them."

"I won't have to tell them," I said. "Someone who drinks at the Empire will. Someone will come in and say, 'Hey Doc, I see your daughter's working as a barmaid down at Ruby's.' I bet that happens—and then you watch out. He'll kill you, Jules." It felt good to be warning her for once.

"I won't be a barmaid. I'm too young. You have to be eighteen to be a barmaid. I'm only waitressing. Just doing tables, Ruby said. Besides, if I like it, I'm going to tell him myself. Tonight."

I took this to be a giant lie, made up on the spot. Asking our father for anything was never easy, but at night, especially after a bad day, it was downright dangerous. "Can I listen?" I said, thoroughly enjoying myself.

Julia pulled a face. "Well, hoo hoo to you, mommy's little darling. Not everyone is as scared of him as you. I guarantee I get away with it. Just you wait and see." She got up, tugging at the dress.

I couldn't let her go, not so easily. "What say someone sees you leaving the house wearing that?"

She gave me a condescending look. "I'm getting changed at the pub, stupid. I'm taking the uniform in a bag, all folded up. And besides, it won't look like a nurse's uniform when I put an apron over it. The other waitresses wear those frilly French ones."

Later I heard her heels click-clacking down the stairs. I guessed she was wearing her silver stilettos.

About lunchtime my mother called me and asked where Julia was.

"In town," I answered truthfully, and she didn't query that. At two-thirty I heard the sound of those heels again, and Julia breezed into my room. She was smiling and her eyes were bright with excitement. She carried two shopping bags, both stuffed with groceries.

"Kimmy," she began, dumping the bags on the floor, "I've had the best time. Ruby is a doll. She runs that place like clockwork." She kicked off her shoes and flopped onto my bed. "When I got there she took me into her office—*her* office, mind you—not his, whatever his name is . . ."

"Hamish," I said.

"Well, Hamish doesn't wear the pants at the Empire, Ruby does. She called me in and said, 'Sit down, Julia,' just like that. She was wearing a dress the color of emeralds—this beautiful green. Around her neck was a gold chain, and on her wrist, and she had this gold ring . . ." here she held out her right hand, ". . . that had the biggest ruby I've ever seen. I said, 'That's a beautiful ring,' and she looked at it like this," here Julia looked nonchalantly at her own fingers, "then she said, 'Oh yes,' very casual, like it was a lump of glass."

"It might have been," I said. Our mother described Ruby's getups as "loud."

Julia sat up, glaring. "I don't care what you think. You weren't even there. I'm telling you that she was very nice to me. She treated me like an adult—which is more than they do around here. Anyway, she took me out into the dining room and showed me around. I got an apron, exactly like the French one I said, then she got me started with Angelo in the kitchen. I did the potatoes, then the carrots, then the—"

This was too much for me. "Julia," I said, "I don't believe this. You never do anything in the kitchen here. You hate cooking. You said—"

"Pooh to whatever I said. I'm not talking about working in a kitchen anyhow. I want a job like Ruby's, running my own business. And it doesn't hurt to learn from the ground up. That's what she did. She told me herself." She relaxed again and turned to face me. "You know what I was thinking coming home? I was thinking about Bobby's. We could turn his place into a sort of country club. One of those resorts where city people come to get back to nature. His place goes right down to the water now the dam's come up. Skiing. Canoeing. I was thinking Bobby could do all the maintenance, like that Hamish does, and I could manage the place like Ruby."

I was amazed. "Julia . . ." I began, but she stopped me again. "No. I'm not listening to you. I know what you're going to say, and I'm not going to listen." She slipped off the bed and began walking backward and forward across the room, talking all the while.

"Now," she said, "about tonight. I'm making the dinner. That's what the groceries are for." She paused and nodded in the direction of the shopping bags, still sitting by the door. "Then I'm telling them about working at Ruby's. They'll be so shocked, so impressed, they won't be able to say no."

If she expected me to say something, she was disappointed. I was struck dumb.

"By the way," she said, gathering her things, "this is going to be a proper dinner, at the dining room table. With entrée and dessert and everything. So you have to help."

"Starting when?" I said, seeing the afternoon vanish. "I wanted to finish a drawing."

"You can finish it later. Seeing you're the arty one, it's your job to do the invitations."

"Invitations? There's only us going, isn't there?"

"Yes," she said. "But I want this done properly. I want to impress them—that's the whole point. So, they can come at six. And make sure that they don't come near the kitchen until then either. Or the dining room. I want this to be a surprise."

I couldn't see the logic in this. "It can't be a surprise if they get an invitation," I said. "And another thing. What say the girl has to be fed. What say they have to get her a drink . . ."

She took two steps toward me. I pulled my legs up

onto the bed. "Just get going," she said. "I'll do a tray up for that stupid girl."

Since an order from Julia usually doubled as a threat, I did as I was told.

I made the invitation out of a piece of my new art paper folded into a card. Although I had no idea what we were eating, I drew a chicken on a platter of vegetables on the front. Inside, I wrote:

Miss Julia Marriott cordially invites
Doctor Ivan and Nurse Helen Marriott
of The Laurels, Jericho,
to a Formal Dinner
at the Great Table in Their Own Dining
Room at Six pm [sharp] this Evening.

PS. Do not enter the vicinity of the
Dining Area before the appointed time.

When this was finished I went downstairs. Julia was in the kitchen reading a recipe book. I showed her the invitation.

"Good," she said. "Now you can deliver it."

I hadn't thought of this. No matter how well prepared the dinner might be, or how well received, I suspected there would still be trouble. I had been careful to leave my name off the invitation, except for my initials beside a copyright symbol which I had printed in minute letters on the back to show my ownership of the artwork but not of the dinner itself.

"Deliver it?" I said. "Why should I deliver it? It's your dinner."

Julia raised her eyebrows in a "please-yourself" expression, then returned her attention to the recipe book. I waited. She turned a page carelessly and said, "Just remember, if I don't get to work for Ruby, you don't get anything from me for Christmas."

As usual I was easily convinced.

I checked in the yard to see if there were any cars. There were none, an indication that my parents were temporarily free, so I went through to the office. My mother wasn't there. The examining room was empty too. I knew then that they were with the girl.

The single room was shut but the door of the next room was ajar. I pushed it open. My parents were kneeling on the floor; between them was a blue blanket which they seemed to be fighting over, or at least pulling this way and that. But when I looked properly I saw that there was somebody in the blanket, and that there were scissors in my mother's hands, and masses of yellow hair all over the floor. They were cutting the girl's hair.

I was about to leave when my mother called "Kim," and I went back. My father didn't look; he was too taken up with controlling the struggling blanket, but my mother said, "What? Quickly, is it urgent?"

I shook my head. "It's only a note," I said. "I'll leave it here." There was a sink just inside the door. I balanced the card on the edge of it and left, closing the door behind me.

I went to the kitchen and told Julia what I'd seen. I didn't exaggerate, there was no need to. She listened carefully. I expected that she'd call the dinner off, but the thought didn't cross her mind.

"Well," she said, "since they're having a bad day, that's all the more reason to make them a good meal."

"Maybe," I said, "but that doesn't mean they'll be in the mood to talk about your job."

She shrugged. "They'll come around. Now, set the table."

We never used the dining room because the cedar table was too big. It could seat twelve people: Five down each side and one at each end. I couldn't set all of it; that would have been ridiculous. I ran my finger along its dark surface, but stopped when I reached the mark of Loony Pilcher's dagger, dead center at the carver's end. I reached out and touched it, feeling gooseflesh spring up on my arms. I covered this end with a starched linen cloth which was the size of a sail until it was folded.

I used our best china and the silver. I put out four crystal champagne flutes, even though we only had water. My father never drank alcohol, but my mother kept a bottle of sherry "for emergencies."

All of these arrangements were made without mishap, and approved by Julia. "Very good," she commented, pursing her lips. "But it needs something on the table . . . something classy . . . like a posy. A centerpiece."

"You can't have a centerpiece if we're all sitting at one end," I pointed out.

"True," she agreed, considering me with some interest. "Quite true. But since you're so arty, I'm sure you'll think of something."

I went out into the yard and looked for a suitable "posy." We had plenty of carefully mown couch grass and raked gravel paths, but nothing that could be called a garden, except for the vegetable patch that Pa scratched around in when he came over. Next to the cellar window was a self-sown tomato bush, straggly and riddled with mites; an Isabella grape crept over the garage, its fruit too thick skinned and sour to eat; and either side of the front door was a woody camellia as old as the house—even these needed a dose of Epsom salts to make them flower, so Pa said. But then I spotted the perfect thing.

The bleeding heart was a creeper that sprouted from the lawn in our front yard. According to Pa, its botanical name was *Cleredendrum impatiens,* but it was called the bleeding heart because it bore clusters of deep red, heart-shaped flowers.

Pa hated it. When he first came to work at The Laurels he had conscientiously cut it back, even mowing right over it; but it only grew up twice as thick. Finally he gave in and now the vine ranged wild, covering a stretch of wall opposite Julia's window with its fleshy green leaves and scarlet flowers.

I returned to the house for some scissors, but when I reached up to cut the flowers, I felt the gooseflesh creep over me again and turned around, sensing that someone was watching me.

The yard was empty; the curtains were drawn. But when I looked higher, there in the sky above my eyrie hovered an eagle, its wings barely moving as it hung on air. I watched, fascinated, then suddenly it swooped low, banked, and soared higher still to vanish into the clouds which drifted in across the valley.

I looked down. On the lawn by the bleeding heart a little gray mouse sat trembling in the sun. I must have disturbed it with all my poking and prodding in the foliage; now it ran back into the shadow of the house and disappeared between the bricks into the darkness of the cellar.

I cut the vine into manageable lengths and twisted them into a circle, but when I put them on the table and stood back to admire my handiwork, it looked like the wreath on Ma Cossey's coffin. I searched for inspiration. On the mantelpiece stood one of my father's earliest taxidermy subjects: An orange-eyed crow. Its feathers were beginning to fade and droop, but the size was right, and the effect when I stood it in the middle of the green and red bleeding heart was quite dramatic.

Julia was pleased. "I knew you'd come up with something," she said.

I followed her back into the kitchen. There were signs of chopping, slicing, beating, and stirring everywhere. I asked what we were having.

"First," she said, "pumpkin soup, then shepherd's pie and vegetables, and after that, fruit salad—with fresh cream for anyone who wants it."

I was impressed. I thought that she would make something fancy, just to be different, but she hadn't: She knew the plain food that our father liked. She was smart, our Julia.

That night we ate together for the first time since the girl had arrived at the house. My parents came to the dining room on time and Julia was ready; she served them without any fuss. The food was good, even my father admitted, and everything went well until coffee, which Julia served with a selection of chocolates too fine to come from any shop in Jericho—a circumstance that might not have been accidental. My mother noticed at once.

"Julia," she said, "where did these come from? Not the co-op, I'm certain."

"From Ruby Parsons," she said straight out. "She keeps them for special customers at the Empire."

My father was interested. "When did you see Ruby?" he asked. "She hasn't been in."

"I saw her yesterday, at the hotel. She offered me a job waitressing."

"I hope you said 'no.'" He used both hands to steady his coffee cup.

My mother put her cup down, guessing what was coming.

"I didn't," Julia answered. "I went in today for a trial and tomorrow I start work there."

My father's voice was very calm. It was the tone I feared most. "I'll phone Ruby tomorrow," he said. "I don't want you doing that, Julia."

"Why?" Julia asked, her voice as controlled as his own.

He didn't answer.

"Why?" she repeated, more insistently this time.

"That was a wonderful meal," he said. "Thank you both." As he spoke he stood up, pushing his chair back.

My mother reached out and touched his arm. "Answer her," she said.

He moved away from the table and stopped behind Julia. "Because I want you to grow up a lady, that's why."

Julia's face changed. She had been determined; now she was angry. She slipped from her chair and stood to face him. "So what am I now?" she said.

My father tried to avoid her but she stepped in front of him, putting one hand on the table, the other on the back of her chair.

"Go on," she demanded, "what does that make me?"

He looked down at her. "Right now? It makes you a willful young girl who is ruining a very special occasion. That's what it makes you. Will you let me pass?"

She released her hold on the chair and brought both hands up to grip his arms above the elbows. I thought she was going to shake him, like she did to me, but she said, "Will you listen? Please. Will you just stop and listen?"

"Ivan," my mother said. "For heaven's sake . . ."

He pulled away and sat down in Julia's chair. He didn't seem angry—more tired, I thought.

"I'm listening," he said.

Julia was standing over him now; she folded her arms and took a deep breath. "I already told Kimmy all this, but I want both of you to know. I didn't go to see Ruby; she saw me. That's the first thing. She asked me what I was doing in the holidays and when I said nothing, she asked me to work on tables until Christmas, and maybe even until New Year. I don't go near the public bar. My job's got nothing to do with alcohol. Ruby has a drink waiter for that. I wear a white uniform and a white apron that Ruby supplies. I used one of your uniforms, Mom—so I was being a lady. I won't embarrass you. It's just an ordinary holiday job . . . like other kids do . . . and I can't see why I'm not allowed to do it."

Throughout this speech my mother had watched Julia intently; my father stared at the crow. When it was finished my mother glanced at him, waiting for a response, but he said nothing.

She sighed. "Julia, give us a chance to talk about this.

I understand what you mean, but a hotel is a hotel, you know, and not really a place for—"

Julia didn't wait for her to finish. "—for a young lady?" she said.

My mother's voice tightened. "I was going to say, for a girl going away to boarding school. But I suppose that's just as bad in your opinion."

Julia never missed an opportunity. She moved suddenly, making even my father jump, and stood at the head of the table. "I don't want to go to boarding school," she said. "I don't want to get locked up in some snooty girls' school. I want to be like Ruby, to learn how to manage a place, like she does. She's her own boss—she's in charge—and she never went to any girls' school. Nobody forced her into doing any stupid la-de-da course in Latin or Religion. You're turning me into a big fake, that's what you're doing, don't you see?"

My father got up a second time. "Have you finished?" he asked.

She stared at him, waiting for more.

"Good," he said. "I'll phone Ruby tomorrow. If what you say about the waitressing is true, then you can keep the job. On the issue of school, there's no debate. You're going."

That was the end of the family dinner—except that when my parents went back to the girl and Julia went up to her room, I was left to do the dishes.

The next morning after breakfast my father called Julia into the living room. My mother took her coffee and joined them. I wasn't asked, but I hung about the doorway long enough to overhear what went on.

"I've phoned Ruby," he began, "and she confirmed what you told us last night. I also talked with your mother. We agree to let you work, but there are a few things that we'd like to make clear to you."

I heard a chair scrape and guessed it would be Julia squirming.

"This job at the Empire is strictly short-term. It stops at Christmas; don't get any ideas about working on into the New Year, even if Ruby offers. Your mother would like you to spend some time with her, especially since you're going away . . . which is the next thing. You *are* going to boarding school. I realize that Ruby has impressed you, and I can understand why. I admire her too, it might interest you to know—and I've known her a lot longer than you have—but you're our daughter, not hers, and until you reach an age where you can live independently, you will do what we say. That's our parental responsibility. That's how we show we love you. Is that clear?"

Julia didn't answer.

"Finally, there's the matter of Kimmy. You're his only sister, his big sister. You should set an example for him . . . but what sort of a model are you providing with your back talk and rudeness? Next time you start one of your little turns, ask yourself that."

There was silence and I was about to disappear when I heard her say, all in a rush, "I am a good model for him. If it wasn't for me, he'd be the—"

"We're not here to talk about Kimmy," my mother broke in. "Now, do you understand what your father's telling you?"

I'd heard enough and went quietly up to my room.

Later Julia came in to see me. She stood beside me at my desk but I didn't bother to look up. "Kimmy," she said, "I'm sorry I didn't help clean up last night. I was going to do it this morning but you already beat me to it. Thanks."

I said that was okay.

"And thanks for that centerpiece too. I wish I had a camera."

Not long after, I heard her leave for work.

I stayed in my room for the rest of that day, except for an occasional visit to the kitchen for food. In the afternoon I was sitting on the back step eating a sandwich when the Fergusons' truck pulled into our yard. Mr. and Mrs. Ferguson went into the house, but Keithy came over to me. After I'd given him a drink—"the last for the day," he said—he got onto the subject I dreaded most.

"Kimbo," he confided, "you shouldn't have told those kids all the stuff you did. It was all bullshit. You Townies, you'd believe anything, I reckon."

"I thought you'd get into trouble," I admitted. "I was worried about that."

He shrugged. "Well, I wet your bed, didn't I? So call us even."

I accepted this as reasonable and asked him if he'd like to come up and see my fossils, since he hadn't the other night. "Sure," he said. "My mom and dad came out for a gasbag with your mom. They'll be ages. But they won't leave me on the farm by myself anymore; not now they know that other one's hanging around."

"Have you seen him again?" I asked, still not having learned to leave a subject well enough alone.

"Nah. He hasn't been back. Not to our place, anyway. But I heard a few things."

"Like?"

"Well, since those rumors started, there's been a couple of parties out after him."

Keithy needed to be coaxed into a talking mood. "Who?" I said. "Which parties?"

"Well . . . I heard that crazy Stafford was one. The one they reckoned shot his mouth off at the inquest."

I was on dangerous ground here. I couldn't admit that I knew more about Stafford than he did, having heard him testify.

"Why?" I said, remaining suitably vague. "What's he after him for?"

"To clear his name. Well, that's what my parents reckon. They reckon he's been copping hell from the workers up the dam since the inquest. He's supposed to be the last one to see Flannagan alive and it was him who heard noises in the bush, right next to the body. So . . . anyway, he's one party. Then another one is Ben Cullen. But he's always up that way, snooping about. We see him lots of times when we're out on the fences. And my dad says he's seen others. . . ."

"That Ben Cullen's an idiot," I said, sounding informed. "I bet he doesn't find anything. That's what Bobby O'Meara says."

Keithy wasn't interested in my fossils. "They look like a pile of rocks to me," he said. "And they're not even rare. There's thousands of shells on our land. We had a snail plague last September when the water came up, and my dad sprayed them. Now there's all these empty shells; so many you squash them when you walk."

I tried to tell him that my shells weren't from land snails, they were fossilized marine shells from the Cambrian period, over 500 million years ago, when even the mountains around Jericho had been buried beneath the sea.

"Sure," he said, "and it's going to happen again if the water in that dam keeps coming up."

Keithy was much more interested in my stamps. He picked up each album and examined it, even asking me to show him a series on agriculture in the United States under my magnifying lens.

"Very interesting," he said, replacing each stamp in its correct pocket.

When he had finished looking I asked him if he'd like another drink. "No," he said, "I better not. But I wouldn't mind some cake. I enjoyed that piece the other night."

I said that we didn't have any cake. My mother hadn't had time to bake—I cut short on giving the reason why, since the girl was supposed to be gone—and offered him a biscuit instead. We were at the head of the stairs. He hesitated as if he was making up his mind, then he turned to me suddenly and said, "No. Don't worry about a biscuit, but if you want to do me a favor, could I see in your sister's room?"

"What? Julia's room?" I said, as if I had another sister hidden away somewhere.

"I've never been in a girl's bedroom before. I wouldn't touch anything. I'd just like to look."

Julia's door was open but he paused before he went in. "You sure this is okay?" he asked.

I nodded. Julia was at work. Unless Keithy wet the bed, she'd never know.

He went in and looked about, then lifted his head to sniff. "It sure smells terrific in here. What would you call that smell?"

I guessed that he meant Julia's Sandalwood. "You call that a fragrance, not a smell," I corrected him. "It's polite to say 'fragrance' when you talk about a woman; like you should say, 'Horses sweat, men perspire, women glow.'"

He looked at me as if I was crazy. "Who told you that?" he said. "Horses froth; that's what horses do. And men stink. You should get a whiff of my dad when he comes in from the pigs."

He was beside Julia's bed by this time, touching the gold brocade of her bedspread. On her bedside table she had a notebook and pencil where she sometimes scribbled addresses and phone numbers. He touched that too.

"That's Julia's personal diary," I said. "No one is allowed to open that."

He looked at me wide-eyed. When he came to her dressing table and saw her makeup, he sniffed again.

"Holy dooly," he sighed. "That is one beautiful fragrance." He stroked the back of Julia's silver brush and removed the lid of a lipstick that she had tossed there. But when he saw the Spanish dancer in her jewelry box, he knelt down and stared in wonder.

"When we were in second grade, Miss Butcher read us a book about a dancing girl. You remember, Kimmy? The story where she loves this tin soldier who gets washed down the gutter." He got up and took a last look around. "Thanks," he said. "I truly appreciate that."

I made myself a drink and found him a biscuit, then we sat on the step and waited for his parents. He asked if I'd heard any news about the girl since she'd been taken away. I shook my head. "I don't get told much anymore," I lied. "Not after what I did last time."

He took another bite of his biscuit. "Well," he said, munching, "we all make mistakes."

eleven

the next day was very quiet. Julia went to work at the Empire and my father had morning house calls, which left just my mother and myself at home. She was busy with the monthly accounts for the practice, as well as looking after the girl. I was glad to have my rubbings to work on; but by midmorning I was sick of my room and took the *Guide to the Stone Ages* up into my tree.

I lay flat, the way I liked, and soon became so comfortable that I forgot about reading and stared out over the valley. I wondered about the boy out there and what he might be doing; he could be hunting, as I had seen him that rainy night of the Spring Dance; or he might be in a tree, exactly like I was, lying still and thinking: About his sister maybe, and if she was safe. I wondered whether he missed her, like I would miss Julia when she was gone.

Just when I was beginning to feel sorry for myself, my book shifted with the wind. I tried to grab it but overbalanced and fell. I hit the wall first, then landed on the lawn. I wasn't hurt, not seriously, but there was enough blood oozing from my knee to justify breaking the "Do Not Disturb" ban imposed by my mother. I picked up my book and went into the house.

I hoped that she might be in the reception room doing the books, but there was no sign of her and I limped down to the girl's room. The door was open and I saw my mother working at a table; the light from the barred window fell directly on the accounts stacked all around her. As soon as I appeared she called me in. I expected to see the girl, but the two beds were made up and empty and, unless she was beneath one of them, or behind the screen that hid the toilet, I couldn't imagine where she was.

"What on earth have you done?" my mother whispered, inspecting my knee. I opened my mouth to answer but before I could, she covered it with her fingers and stared first at me, then over my shoulder. I turned to look. Behind the door, propped up in a corner, was the bundle of blue blanket that I had seen the previous Sunday. Judging from its bulk, and a shadowy opening where a face should be, I guessed that the girl was wrapped inside.

I raised my eyebrows as if to say, *Is that her?*

My mother nodded. "I'll get something to put on that knee," she said and before I could protest she left the room.

Not taking any chances, I sat at the table and faced the girl. The trickle of blood had now reached my shin, but I daren't take my eyes off her to wipe it away. I could see that she was watching me too—I could make out her pale eyes—and we sat like two cats staring over a saucer of milk.

My mother came back with the iodine and some dressing. I put my leg out and she knelt down to attend to it.

"There," she said. "Now, have a walk to see if that bandage is too tight."

I walked to the toilet screen and back, passing right in front of the girl. Even though I came so close, she didn't look away.

"Good," my mother said. "Now, how about you go up to your room and give that leg a rest for a while?"

I didn't want to go. The girl fascinated me; I wanted to see her properly. I got as far as the reception room and hung about there, flicking through magazines I had read a thousand times before, and next thing I was back in the room.

"Could I stay here?" I asked, looking as miserable as possible. "I'll be quiet, and I've got a book." This was true. My book about the Stone Ages was on the table.

"You can if you like," she said. "I'll be here for a while. Lie on one of those beds . . ." Then she added pointedly, "Nobody else seems to want to."

This was an excellent idea. I had company and I could watch the girl. I picked up my book and got settled.

After I had pretended to read for a while I realized that the girl had no intention of doing anything of interest. In fact she had made no sound or movement at all, and from where I was, at the other end of the room, I couldn't even distinguish her eyes, let alone tell if she was watching me.

I went over to my mother. "I'll only be a minute," I said. "I need some things from my room."

I came back with a box of crayons, some sheets of art paper, and the fossils that Bobby had found.

"Where are you going to put that?" my mother said.

"Here," I answered, and deliberately spread the paper on the floor between her table and the girl. My mother ignored me, but the girl didn't.

As soon as I began drawing I could tell that she watched every mark I made. I traced the shape of the stone that contained the fossil, then I began to draw the pattern free-hand. These drawings weren't intended for my mother for

Christmas, so it didn't matter if she saw what I was doing, but the more I drew the more I exaggerated the difficulty of the task. I picked up and rejected crayons. I sat back and sighed. Pretending that I needed to catch some elusive source of light, I held the sheet up just high enough for her to see what I had done. All in all, I showed off.

This demonstration might have gone on for some time if my mother hadn't left the room to answer the phone in the reception room.

As soon as I was alone my creativity vanished. I panicked. I scrambled over the floor picking up crayons and fossils and putting them away, but as I reached out to roll up my paper, I realized that I was too late. The girl had begun to move.

She pulled herself along, using her concealed hands to drag the blanket over the floor. When she reached the drawing she extended one arm to balance herself. The blanket fell from her head and shoulders and for the first time, I saw her.

Her yellow hair was cut short and uneven, the exact opposite of Julia's; her ears stuck out like a creature's in a fairy story. Her face was thin and her chin sharp. When she looked at me, her eyes caught the sunlight from the window and shone blue as day.

She didn't seem to be frightened of me at all. She leaned forward and pulled the drawing to her, inspecting it carefully. She picked up the fossil that I had copied and compared it to the drawing. Then, looking at me again, she said, "This drawing's that shell."

I drew back beneath the table.

She wasn't worried. "Where'd you get this?" she said, holding the fossil out toward me.

I shook my head.

"From up the Thumbs?"

"Our friend Bobby found it," I said, finding my voice.

"Up the Thumbs?" she persisted.

I nodded.

"There's plenty of these up the Thumbs. And bones. Bats' bones in the caves . . ." She turned the fossil in her hands, then she said, "Is she your mother, that nurse?"

I nodded again.

"She done this to my hair." She ran her hand through it. "I spat at her. I spat at him too, and bit him. That doctor bastard."

"That's my father," I said and, feeling braver, "he stitched up your father's arm."

She looked at me carefully when I said that.

"Your father came here with two blue parrots. We had to bury them, my sister Julia and me. You were in the back of a pickup, and we gave some peppermint to you and that boy."

At the mention of her brother, she looked up at the window. "Micky's out there," she whispered.

I crept a bit closer. "Is Micky your brother?"

She returned her attention to the drawing.

"My name's Kim," I said, moving closer still. "Your brother's name, and mine, they're nearly the same if you turn them around. Kimmy and Micky. See?"

She studied the drawing harder. I said, "Is your name Colleen?"

She glared at me and I drew my legs up. "Your mother called me that. I hate that name. You call me Leena." She began fiddling with a crayon.

"You can draw something if you want to," I said. "I was only playing around."

She checked to see if I meant it. When I nodded, she rubbed the crayon on the paper, making a bright red mark. She smiled. "When I went to school I used to draw pictures. And read. I could read a book—the same as you, when you sat up there . . ." She glanced in the direction of the bed. As she did, she saw my mother at the door.

"Mom . . ." I began, trying to keep her away, but she had already come in.

Leena shifted toward the corner, taking the blanket with her.

My mother bent down and whispered to me. "You're doing a good job. I'll take my things into the reception room, okay?" She picked up her books and left. Leena watched every move.

"She's gone," I said. "I can shut the door if you like." She didn't answer so I got up and pushed it closed. When I looked back Leena had already returned to the paper.

Throughout that afternoon she sat on the floor drawing. She worked on a corner of the paper for ages, making tiny geometric shapes and then coloring them in. Sometimes she spoke, but only to ask if what she had done was good, or for me to help her peel back the paper wrapped around the crayons; her fingernails were too short and split to be much use.

Once she got up and said, "I have to pee." She didn't ask me to leave, so I waited. She limped across to the screen and I saw her bandaged ankle for the first time.

Much later my mother brought drinks and biscuits

and, just before dinner, Julia appeared. She walked right in and perched on a corner of the table.

"Are you all right?" she said.

I said that I was and made signs for her to leave. She couldn't have misunderstood but she wouldn't go.

"Aren't you going to introduce me?" she asked, grinning.

"This is Leena. She knows who you are. I already told her."

Julia couldn't resist showing off. "I've been working at the pub," she said, looking over my head and speaking directly to Leena. "I've got a waitressing job there."

Leena turned her head toward the corner.

Julia persisted. "So. Can I get you something? A drink or something?"

I told her we'd had that. She shrugged. "I'm just trying to be sociable," she said, crossing her legs and showing off her silver shoes.

I got up. "You're not fair," I whispered. "I'm the first person she's talked to and it's going all right. Don't be horrible and muck it all up."

She made a face as if to say, *Who me?* then slipped off the table. "Well," she said, "it seems that I'm not wanted." She click-clacked out of the room.

My father came in after he had finished his calls. He nodded and smiled when he saw us sitting on the floor with the drawings. Leena ignored him. She was too busy with her coloring in, but I felt very proud.

From that day on, until Christmas when everything changed, I spent most of my time with Leena.

twelve

leena wore dresses belonging to my mother, and when she wasn't in one of her moods, wrapped up in her blanket, I could see the cuts and scratches on her arms and legs. Some of these had healed, but most were purple scars. My mother said she doubted they would ever fade. There was one scar across her arm, just above the elbow, that looked as if it had been made by a saw. I asked her about it. "Ran into a barbwire fence," she said, "years ago, when Fadder was a rabbiter." "Fadder" was the name she called Paddy Flannagan; she never called him "dad" or "father."

There were red lumps behind her ears and on the back of her neck, and sometimes she would stop whatever she was doing to scratch them. I asked her if my father had had a look at them. She shrugged. "They're nothin'. They're just what's left of bush ticks. Bloodsucking buggers. They make you sick if you don't pull them out, real sick."

"What?" I said. "Did you get them out yourself?"

She gave me a funny look. "No. You can't do it yourself. You get someone else to do it."

"So who will do Micky's now you've gone?"

"He'll be all right," she mumbled, and that was the end of that—for the time being.

The first drawings Leena did were geometric shapes repeated over and over until an entire sheet of paper had been covered. A finished sheet looked like a patchwork quilt, and when I pinned it on the wall she thought I was terrific.

One morning I was late coming down to see her. When I arrived she was working on a different kind of drawing that seemed to be a group of gray and black towers with turrets and windows.

"Is that a castle?" I asked.

She lifted her crayon from the page and looked at me as if I was stupid. "A castle? I wouldn't draw a castle. It's the Thumbs, see? There's the caves and there's the big rocks near the top."

Leena also liked books. She didn't care what they were about, provided they had pictures, and she loved to hear me read aloud. She would shift her position until she sat in front of me, then she sounded out the words that I read, touching her lips with her fingertips. That was how I discovered another of her secrets: She couldn't read.

On the third day I was with her, "Mister" paid Leena his first visit. I'd been in the yard talking to the sergeant but when I went back to the room I couldn't see her. I found her curled up in her blanket behind the door, just as she had been on the first day. She was looking up at the window. I looked up too.

"What's up there?" I said, kneeling in front of her. "What can you see?"

She whispered something that I couldn't understand.

"I can't hear you," I said. "What's wrong?"

"Mister," she said very clearly.

"Mister," I repeated. "Mister who?"

"Out there," she said. "Mister's out there."

I laughed. "It's only the sergeant. He came to see my parents."

No amount of reassurance would calm her, nor would she get up to look for herself, so finally I left her alone, thinking she was in one of her moods.

But the problem wasn't that simple. As the days passed I often found Leena in the corner muttering that name, "Mister," and though I tried to get out of her who he was, or what he wanted, I never could.

Apart from the time that I spent with Leena, I kept up my work on the fossil rubbings for my mother's Christmas present, and when Pa came to do the yard they were finished and ready to frame, as promised.

I was with Leena when he turned up. "Pa's here," my mother said, "and he says he has to see you."

"I have to go for a while," I explained to Leena. "There's a man who wants to see me."

She was looking at a copy of the *Australian Women's Weekly,* a magazine that could keep her engrossed for hours. She couldn't have cared less that I was going.

I met Pa in the reception room. "It's nearly that time," he said, and gave me a sly wink, because my mother was at the desk listening.

I led him outside into the yard. "I'm sorry I kept you waiting," I said, "but I was in with the girl." The words were out before I could stop myself.

"What girl?" he said.

"No one," I mumbled. "Just a girl." I couldn't lie like Julia.

He stopped. "What girl?" he asked again. His smile had gone.

I couldn't think.

"Not the Flannagan girl?"

I nodded.

"Well, well," he said. "There you go. A secret, hey?"

"Please Pa," I begged, "I wasn't supposed to say. She's been here all the time. I'll get killed if they find out. . . ."

We had been walking toward the vegetable garden, but now he looked back toward the house. "Which room?" he asked. "Not the same one as Ma?"

He meant the room Ma Cossey had died in.

"No. The double one." I pointed. "The window at the end."

He shaded his eyes and stared as if he had never seen this part of the house before.

"That window got bars?" he asked.

"All the ground floor windows are barred." He knew that.

"Can she see out?"

"No," I said, "not unless she climbed up on something."

He shook his head and walked on.

"Pa," I said, running to catch up with him, "you won't tell, will you?"

He didn't answer. When we reached the garden he bent down and pulled out a few thistles, tossing them against the wall. I tried a different subject.

"I finished the rubbings," I said. "They're inside, all wrapped up ready."

He grunted and stood up, arching his back the way he did if he had been sitting or bending. "Well," he said, "you'd better show me what you've done, then I can get on and do my bit."

I left him in the kitchen and went upstairs to get the rubbings, but when I came back he wasn't there. He'd gone outside again and was staring up at Leena's window. I called him and he waved. "Okay, okay," he said. "Just looking at this place. That guttering up there looks like it's new."

A plumber had replaced our guttering after all the rain in September, and Pa had seen it before, I was certain. I remembered my father discussing quotes with him before it was painted—but I didn't say so and he followed me back into the kitchen.

I spread the rubbings on the table. He undid the buttoned-down flap of his shirt pocket and took out the purple-lined case that held his reading glasses. He handled the case as if it contained a precious instrument, removed the glasses with great care and positioned them exactly on the tip of his nose. He cleared his throat, pulled back his sleeves and picked up the first drawing, then the second, then the third and the fourth.

"Yep," he said. "Yep. They're good. These will do up fine. And that's quality paper you've used. No point in making a good solid frame if the paper's rubbish. It goes yellow and brittle, then it's useless. Now, about these frames. I've got some packing-case pine on my bench that would do these proud, when I plane it back and varnish it up. How about that? They'd be honey-colored pine."

I said that sounded good but he heard something in my voice and said, "Come on, out with it."

"They will have glass, won't they?" I asked. "Glass over the front?"

"Glass? Of course they'll have glass. I've got old windows there that I scrounged when they demolished Pitt's service station for the dam runoff, out on Fraser's Road. They'll have glass, all right."

"And will they be finished by Christmas?"

"By Christmas Eve. That's when you need them. Yep. If it's for your mom, they'll be done. I'll bring them in with your tree."

It was tradition that every Christmas Eve he brought us a pine sapling to set up as our Christmas tree.

I went back to Leena's room when Pa had gone. The door was closed, but I opened it, calling "It's only me." Magazines were scattered on the floor but there was no sign of her. I looked behind the door and there she was, wrapped up in her blanket. I guessed what was wrong.

"Mister," was all she said.

"Where?" I said, staring about. "I don't see anyone."

"Out there," she said, looking at the window.

I knelt in front of her. "Nobody's out there," I said, "I was just out there myself. There's not even a car."

I was blocking her line of sight and she pushed me away.

"You're crazy," I said, getting up. "You can stay here by yourself." I walked out and slammed the door.

I went into the reception room and sat on the settee.

"What's going on?" my mother asked.

"Mister's back," I explained.

She groaned; she'd heard about Mister. "It has to mean something," she said. "But her life's been such a mess, we might never know. How would you like to live with the thought that your father's murderer is still out there, free as a bird? It's no wonder she acts the way she does."

"Do you think she knows who killed him?"

"The sergeant doesn't seem to think so, and he's tried to get it out of her. But there's some people from welfare coming to see her, before Christmas, I'm told."

"Will they take her away?" I said.

She thought about that. "Well, it's not easy for any of us having her here. Julia won't go near her, for reasons that I don't understand. . . ."

"Julia's a pain. She just wants to be—"

She wouldn't listen. "Let's not go into that. Julia is Julia, I know, but she lives in this house too . . . though I have to admit that since Leena came, neither of you have had much attention."

"But they'd put her in a girls' home, wouldn't they?"

"I don't know about that; she's on a very short fuse, and things like this Mister business, well, that just can't go on. . . ."

Christmas Day fell midweek that year, and on the Monday morning before, my mother said, "You had better keep out of the yard today. There's a special delivery due."

I knew exactly what she meant: The presents that she had put away months before were being delivered from the city.

I laughed, "Oh, so the Christmas presents are coming, are they?"

"Very smart, aren't we?" she said.

"And does that mean my present is too big to wrap up, or too hard to disguise?"

"It could have nothing to do with you. It could be Julia's present that I don't want you to see."

"Why? I wouldn't tell her."

She laughed. "Your track record isn't so good on that score, is it?"

It was worse than she knew.

I went down to Leena and busied myself with a new project. Now that the fossil rubbings were finished, I was teaching Leena to read. She had been to school, I worked that out from the stories that she told me about her teachers, but just how many schools was hard to say— except that there must have been plenty. Her father had shifted from place to place, mostly in the country— though she might have lived in a city once. When she saw pictures of high-rise buildings (any high-rise buildings in any city anywhere) she would say, "We went there," or "Fadder took us there."

Once I asked, "Did you live there?" but she wouldn't answer. Another time she saw a picture of a convict looking through a barred window in a jail cell. She looked at this for a long time.

I said, "Is that Mister?"

She shook her head. "No, that's where the Fadder was." I guessed that Flannagan had spent some time in jail.

The problem with teaching Leena to read was that she pretended she already could and I knew she couldn't— though I didn't let on. This made teaching her very difficult; but nothing I couldn't handle, I thought.

I devised a plan to draw an alphabet chart. I told Leena that it was for the Jericho Preschool, and I was doing it over the holidays to have ready for the first day back. Every letter had to be shown and each of these needed both a word and an object beginning with that letter to appear beside it. I said that we didn't have to draw all this ourselves, we could cut the letters and pictures out of magazines, but she said no; she wanted to draw everything.

Leena knew the letters and their sounds, which was a start, but when it came to finding a word to fit the sound and then being able to draw a picture to fit the word, things became complicated. But we began well. For *A*, Leena chose the word *ant;* these insects had plagued her when she was in the bush. *B* was for *bat,* since these lived in the *C* for *caves.*

"Did you live in a cave?"

As usual when she didn't want to answer, she went on with her coloring.

While I was very involved in helping Leena and happy to watch her draw, all that morning I kept my ears open for the arrival of a truck. After years of hearing patients drive into our yard, I had become an expert on the engine noises of all sorts of vehicles and the different sounds their tires made on our gravel drive. I could tell my father's car without looking.

About ten-thirty I heard what I thought was a possibility enter the yard. I opened the door and listened along the corridor to hear who my mother greeted. It was a false alarm, only Florence Steele who had come to collect a prescription in her son's pickup. No sooner had she left than there was another, so much the same that I thought it was Florence come back and didn't bother going out—but when I heard the squeak of a metal door opening and something heavy being unloaded, I looked up and listened. Leena looked up too, and as she did I heard footsteps on the gravel below the window.

"Mister," she said. "That's Mister," and she reached for her blanket.

I dragged the table over to the window and climbed onto it. There was a delivery van and, leaning against it, a brand new bike, glinting silver in the sun.

As I looked a man with a clipboard appeared, his boots crunching on the gravel. That was when I made the "Mister" connection. It was boots—the sound of a man's boots on gravel. The same sound the sergeant had made, and Pa, and who knows what other visitors?

I turned to Leena but she was already in her corner, the blanket wrapped tight around her.

"It's nobody," I said, "come and see. Quick. It's just footsteps on the gravel. That's all. Just someone's boots on the gravel. It's nothing to be frightened of."

I was wasting my time. She was muttering and swearing beneath her breath, wide-eyed with terror.

I had discovered one of the secrets of Mister—but not the most important; I had also seen my Christmas present, I was certain, which was both good and bad.

thirteen

the sergeant arrived with the welfare people on Christmas Eve. My mother had given up on them, thinking that they had left the visit so late that they wouldn't be coming, at least not before Christmas.

They were both women, dressed in suits and carrying briefcases. One was a doctor, Dr. Tiffin—much younger than my father—and the other was a social worker, Ms. Cuttler. It seemed that they were too important to have first names, but Julia would have named them in a minute: Dr. Tiffin would be Jennifer—Jenny to her friends—Ms. Cuttler would be Dagmar or Bertha. She had a face you could strike a match on, my mother said.

We had no chance of warning Leena that they were coming. We had intended to tell her the day before, not to stir her up too much, but now it was too late. My mother took me aside and whispered, "Get in there and tell Leena she's having visitors. And make sure that she's got a dress on, not a nightie . . . and that she hasn't got breakfast all over her face. . . ."

When I told Leena what was happening I thought she'd throw a tantrum, but she didn't. She said, "Will they take me away?" in a quiet, matter-of-fact voice.

I admitted that I didn't know, that it all depended on her, and whether she behaved and answered their questions.

"Do you want me to stay?" she said.

I said that I did.

"For how long?"

I didn't know what to say. I didn't want trouble with everyone sitting right next door. Finally I came up with, "For as long as you like." She seemed pleased with that.

The interview was held in the room beside Leena's. My mother and I sat through it all but my father came and went. He had patients and refused to turn them away without notice. He pointed this out to Dr. Tiffin and asked that next time she show more professional consideration by making an appointment. She didn't like that much.

Each woman had her own particular line of inquiry: Was the girl eating, was she sleeping, was she on medication, was she violent, how was she occupying her time—they went on and on until the doctor said, "I now have some personal questions. I wonder if . . ." She looked at my mother, then at me, suggesting that the time had come for me to leave.

"Ask away," my mother said. "Growing up with the office in the house, there's very little that Kim hasn't seen or heard."

I was surprised to hear this. Certainly Julia and I had seen our share of naked bodies about the office, but what really mattered, like sexual intercourse, I'd put together from reading the pharmaceutical catalog. I couldn't say the same for Julia.

Ms. Cuttler sniffed in disapproval but the doctor went on: "Has the girl menstruated?" she asked.

"No," my mother said, "but then she's only been here two weeks; and stress could explain—"

Dr. Tiffin broke in. "A simple no would be sufficient,

Nurse. I'm aware of the effects of trauma on menstruation. Next, your husband forwarded me a copy of his medical examination undertaken shortly after the girl arrived. This was quite thorough. However, he failed to mention whether or not the girl had undergone an internal examination. Has such an examination been undertaken, do you know?"

"No, Ivan hasn't done an internal. Leena was sedated for the first few days, and that allowed us to do the general examination you received, but to do an internal, she would've needed to be fully anesthetized; that was the extent of her resistance. Besides, we had no authority to proceed with that—and what would have been the point? She showed no signs of having been molested, and whether she was a virgin or not was none of our business."

Ms. Cuttler twisted in her chair. "Mrs. Marriott—" she began.

"Nurse," my mother corrected.

"Nurse Marriott, we're not in the habit of discussing this type of thing in front of children."

"I have given you my opinion on that," my mother reminded her.

Ms. Cuttler sniffed again. "Very well. I hope that no embarrassment is caused. We are concerned here about the possibilities of sexual abuse. Do you realize that?"

"Sexual abuse? Who was there to abuse her?"

"Her father, for one."

"Her father? He was murdered ten months ago. Whatever happened or didn't happen between them is not going to be evident now."

"There are plenty of other men around, I'm sure," Ms. Cuttler concluded, with a hasty glance about the room.

"But she hasn't seen a human being for months."

"Isn't there a brother?" Ms. Cuttler whispered, with a touch of triumph.

My mother sighed. "From all reports, her brother is a child, no older than Kimmy here. Make what you like of that, but I think this is all really pointless. Leena may or may not have had intercourse. She's had a terrible life from what we've been able to learn—and she may or may not have been sexually abused by any number of people as a result. But not recently. If she's pregnant, and I see no evidence that she is, I can't imagine who would be responsible. But if you want to pursue the issue, that's entirely up to you."

So the questions went on. My mother answered most of them although sometimes she would say, "Kim can answer that better than I can," or "Kim knows more about that than I do."

Ms. Cuttler was not impressed.

When the time came, Leena spoke for herself. She was polite to the women when my mother introduced them, but when she saw the sergeant she stiffened and turned to the wall.

"She doesn't like me much," he said. "I'm the one who brought her here. I'd better wait outside."

Ms. Cuttler was about to protest but Dr. Tiffin stopped her. "Let him go," I heard her say.

Leena and I sat on the floor next to the alphabet chart and my mother stood by the door, ready to assist my father if he called. Our visitors sat at the table to make notes . . . except what Leena told them wasn't worth writing down as far as I was concerned.

She said that she was fifteen years old. She was sure

of that because her last teacher had said so—but just how long ago that was she didn't know. Nor did she know where she was born, except that it was somewhere to the west: "Through the Gate," she said, "that Angel's Gate."

On the subject of her mother she was quite definite: She had blond hair like her own. Or so "the Fadder" had told her.

She insisted that she could read and write and said that was why she was working on the alphabet chart with me—to help children who couldn't. She showed the women the chart to prove this. Both Dr. Tiffin and Ms. Cuttler were sensible enough to pretend to believe her.

Once, when she was a little girl, she was taken to a hospital because she had a bad cough and a fever.

"Did your father take you?" the doctor asked.

"No," Leena answered, "Moira did."

"Who was Moira?"

Leena refused to answer.

Ms. Cuttler changed the subject. "Leena," she began, "where were you when your father died?"

Leena didn't think twice. "In the bush."

"And was your brother with you?"

"Micky was always with me until I came here."

"And did you see who it was who did that awful thing to your father?"

Leena gave her a questioning look. "What awful thing?"

"Why . . . killed him," Ms. Cuttler stammered.

"I already told the cops all about that. We were in the bush, see, and it was dark."

Ms. Cuttler didn't give up. "But your brother, Micky— might he have seen?"

Throughout this, Leena had been holding a crayon, ready to go on with coloring our chart. Now she slammed it down on the floor. "I told you Micky was with me. So if it was dark for me, it was dark for Micky too. Okay?"

Ms. Cuttler took a deep breath. "Leena," she said, "it's part of my job to protect you. If the person who killed your father is still about, he might want to harm you too. And your brother. Do you understand?"

Leena chose another crayon and leaned forward. Ms. Cuttler tried a different approach. "You're safe here, Leena," she said, "but Micky isn't. Micky's still out there. He could be in danger. You wouldn't want anything to happen to Micky, would you?"

When Leena heard this she covered her mouth and laughed. Without even looking up, she said, "You're mad. That's what you are. No one would ever catch Micky." Then she went on with her work. The interview was over.

When they had gone I asked my mother for the verdict.

"They're considering it," she said. "Which means we get to keep her for the time being, because they don't know what else to do with her."

"How long is 'the time being'?" I asked.

She laughed. "I'd say at least until Christmas. . . ."

fourteen

Pa arrived late that afternoon. I saw him coming into the yard and ran to meet him at the kitchen door. He was balancing a pine sapling on his shoulder and carrying a shopping bag.

"Well," he said, "here it is . . . and it's a good one. Plenty of branches, nice and full. I got it from the edge of the forestry estate way up near Fergusons'. There's a few seedlings come up on the wrong side of the fence, so I reckon they don't belong to anyone. You'll be wanting to decorate it tonight, eh?"

I was much more interested in the shopping bag. "It looks like a good tree, Pa," I said. "But what about my pictures? Did you do them?"

He looked about quickly. "Your mother's not likely to come in?"

I shook my head. "She's had people here all day. She's working inside with my father."

He put the bag on the table and removed a brown-paper package tied with string.

"Is that them?" I asked.

"Might be."

"How come they're all done up like that? It looks like you were mailing them overseas."

"No," he said, "something valuable as this deserves to be treated with respect. Now, have a look."

He handed me the package and I sat down to open it.

"The string is too tight," I protested, but before I could get up to find the scissors he produced his pocketknife and cut it.

When the paper was opened I discovered newspaper packing beneath and then the first frame appeared. I lifted it out. It was much better than I had imagined: The corners were square and even, the wood pale, the glass clean and shining. The rubbings looked too good to have been done by me—I was glad that I'd signed them. As I lifted each one out and examined it, I took a quick look at Pa. I could see that he was pleased too.

"Thanks," I said. "These are terrific. I owe you a favor."

"You don't owe me anything. It's Christmas . . . and as a matter of fact, I've got something else here for you."

His hand went into his pocket and he held out another brown-paper parcel, much smaller than the first.

"Sorry I don't have any proper wrapping," he said. "Go on, take it. Merry Christmas, Kimmy."

I took the present from him. It was heavy for something so small. "Should I open it now," I asked, "or should I put it under the tree for tomorrow?"

"Depends. Are you expecting something big tomorrow? Something expensive maybe?"

The bike hadn't been out of my mind since the day I saw it leaning against the van. I guessed that it was down in the cellar, hidden in some dark place where I wouldn't go.

"There's one thing," I admitted. "I'd say it was pretty expensive. And big."

"That's what I thought. In that case, you should open this now . . . before you do, I want you to know this didn't cost anything—but it's still precious. All right?"

I tried to look as if I understood, but I didn't—not until I saw what he had given me, until it lay sparkling in the palm of my hand.

"It's a quartz crystal," he explained, "and a beauty too. I found it in a gravel bed up Traveston way. See the six sides, all equal, and the ends coming to points. That's the characteristics of crystal. But they don't have to be clear, like some people think. They could be smoky gray, or pink—rose quartz they call that—or purple, but that's a step up—that's amethyst, and really a gemstone. But that piece there, it's a beauty. Now, hold it up to the light and tell me what you see."

I held the crystal between my finger and thumb and turned to the door to catch the last light of the sun.

"It's clear," I said, "like glass."

"It is," Pa agreed. "It is. Now turn it. Turn it right over, end for end. There's more, isn't there?"

I turned it again and again. "There's a bubble," I said. "A bubble of something inside."

"It's water, that's what it is. A drop of water. Millions of years ago, a dinosaur splashing around kicked up a little drop that landed right on this crystal—at the very moment it was forming—and the crystal closed over. Sealed it up forever. Trapped it inside. Wonderful, hey? Precious, that's what I say. Precious."

Pa was right; the crystal was a precious thing, as precious as my fossils, I knew, and as I held it to the sun, tipping it this way and that, a wave of guilt came over me. Pa had brought the tree, he had made the frames, he had given me this precious thing, yet I had nothing to give him in return. Nothing. I had forgotten about him completely.

"Pa," I lied, "I would have had something for you, but with the girl here and everything . . ."

He laughed so loudly that I had to stop. "What?" I said. "I mean it, really . . ."

"Kimmy, you just gave me your present. See? Just standing here watching you is my present. That's all the present I want." He began to clean up the paper and string. "Come on, let's get this away before your mother comes in."

I put the crystal on the table and packed the rubbings back in the paper. As I did, he said, "And how's that girl? Is she having Christmas too?"

"I suppose so," I answered. "But she doesn't really know what it's about, I don't think. As far as I can tell she's never had a present before, or anything like that."

"And are you giving her one then?"

"We got her a new nightie, and perfume. And a brush, because her hair is growing back again . . ."

He gave me a strange look. "What does that mean?"

"It was cut short. It was full of knots and had burrs tangled up in it."

"Any ticks?"

"How did you know" I said.

"How did I know? Because it's crawling with those bloodsuckers up there. It's all those cows that they come for . . . But they like a drop of human blood for dessert."

"She didn't have any, not when she came in. She only had red lumps where they'd been."

"Good. That's good to hear. They can poison your blood, you know. They can kill you if the head breaks off in you and gets infected."

When the rubbings were packed I took them up to

my room, then I called my mother to tell her that Pa was there. She came out with my father to wish him a happy Christmas.

After dinner I wanted to decorate the tree and asked if Leena could help.

"Bobby was coming tonight," Julia said. "But he can't if she's out here."

My father was still at the table. "Who said he could come?" he asked, looking at my mother.

"I did," she said. "But I forgot about Leena. What time will he be here, Julia?"

"About nine. After he's picked up some Christmas things for his mother."

"Good. That gives you two hours. All you have to do is get the tree ready and by the time he arrives Leena can be back in her room."

"But Bobby was going to help with the tree," Julia protested.

"Think yourself lucky he's coming at all," my father said, and the argument stopped there.

Julia and I went out to the garage, found a drum to stand the tree in and took it into the house. When it was set up by the living room fireplace, I asked if I should get Leena.

"I don't care," Julia said. "She's not my responsibility."

This was the first time that Leena had been out of her room. She followed me without any trouble, all the while asking questions about the house and looking around everywhere. When she reached the living room and saw Julia, she went quiet.

"Julia's going to help us," I explained.

I can't say that she heard me. She had already spotted

the glass and tinsel decorations that Julia was removing from a carton. Without a word, she dropped to her knees and picked one up, then another and another.

I saw Julia look at her, then hand her one: A plastic doll dressed as an angel with frosted silver wings.

"This goes on the top," she said, pointing up.

Leena took it from her and examined it, holding it in the palm of her hand. After a bit of thought, she said, "Is this a boy or a girl?"

I didn't know.

Julia looked at it carefully, finally lifting its dress. "Well," she said, matter-of-factly, "it hasn't got a willie!"

Leena looked for herself, pulling the dress higher to expose the chest. "And it hasn't got titties either . . ." she said, her face quite serious. ". . . Must be a bloody maph-rodite."

Julia's eyes opened wide as saucers. She looked at Leena; she looked at me. I shrugged again.

Then Leena added, choking on her own giggles, "Hey . . . how would it like a pine tree stuck up its bum!"

There was no trouble with Julia after that.

We were so involved with the tree that none of us saw Bobby arrive. "I'm here," he said from the doorway. Leena saw him and crouched behind the tree, but she moved too late. I saw the shock in his face.

Julia whispered to me, "I'll fix this," and took him out of the room.

I moved around the tree to where Leena was hiding. "It's all right," I said. "That's only Bobby, Julia's friend. I told you about him." I reached up and fixed some loose decorations.

After a few minutes, when she was certain that he had

gone, she stood up. "Is that her boyfriend?" she asked.

I said that it was. She was quiet again, then she said, "Would they be kissing now?"

I told her they would probably be out in the yard, talking. "But *do* they kiss?" she said, handing me a glass ball.

"Sure, but not when people are around."

She thought about that. "And will they get married?"

"They might, but they're too young now. Besides, Julia has to go to boarding school and then university, most likely."

"To be a teacher?"

I laughed. I couldn't imagine Julia being a teacher. "No. Maybe to be a manager."

"Like someone's boss?"

"Yes. Somebody's big boss."

Julia came in just as we were finishing.

"Is everything all right?" I said.

"He's gone," she whispered. "But you won't tell them he saw her, will you?"

I shook my head. It was good to have something on Julia.

When Leena had finally returned to her room, protesting all the way, and I had gone to bed, Julia came in for a talk.

"So," she said, sitting beside me, "what do you think Santa will bring you tomorrow?"

"A bike," and I told her the story of what I had seen from Leena's window.

"Did you ask for a bike?"

"No," I admitted.

She frowned. "I asked for a bike about five years in a

row and I never got one. You don't even ask and you get one anyway. I can't work that out. Maybe it's just me. Maybe they thought it wasn't ladylike to ride a bike."

"Maybe they thought you'd ride away and never come back," I suggested.

"Or maybe it's okay for them to *send* me away—but they don't want me *escaping*."

"Did you ask for anything?" I said.

"Cassettes. All the music I've got is awful."

"Did you get me something?" I prodded, enjoying myself enough to fluff my pillow and sit up.

"I might have." She slipped from the bed to stand beside the window. "There were plenty of nice cheap toys in the co-op. Little bears and rubber ducks and things . . ." She lifted the curtain and peered out into the night.

"Julia," I said, "I warn you. If you start with any scary stuff I'll end up in your room."

She looked back. "What? Scared even on Christmas Eve?"

"I'm never scared. Not any more."

"That's good," she said, "because I know some scary stuff. Bobby told me tonight."

I couldn't tell if she was joking or not. "Julia, I warn you . . ."

She let the curtain fall but she didn't sit down. She walked this way and that, twisting a strand of her hair as she spoke. "Bobby says there's been sightings of the boy in Jericho. In the town. Once in the yard at the back of the depot, once in the park, and once going through the bins behind the Paradise."

"Who said so?"

"Different people."

"Who?" I demanded, not wanting to believe.

"Queenie. She told Bobby that—"

"I wouldn't believe Queenie," I said. "She's the one who reckoned she saw that Yarama thing. I wouldn't believe her."

She stood still. "How do you know about that?" she said.

I had to think fast. "I was in the Paradise when she told you, remember?"

"Well," she said, satisfied, "whether you believe her or not, it makes sense to me."

"How does it make sense?"

"You listen," she said, sitting on the chair at my desk. "First, how old would this kid be? Ten? Twelve?"

"He might be."

"Okay. So let's say we've got a twelve-year-old running around out there all alone. His sister's here, right? It's harder for him to get food now that she's gone, so he comes in closer to people where it's easier to scavenge. He can go through bins, like at the Paradise; he can get what's left of the milk from the cans in the depot yard. How about that?"

I didn't say anything. There was obviously more.

"And then there's her . . . I bet he loves her. Being her little brother, you know. Like you. You'd miss me, wouldn't you? So he's coming in to look for her. That's another reason."

"Why would he look for her here? He doesn't even know where she is!"

"Really?" She said this with a little smile. "You know that for sure, do you?" She pulled her chair closer. "Well, let me tell you something. The other day when you were in there with Leena, I just happened to hear a conversation between our parents and the sergeant. Except it wasn't much of a conversation—it was more like a lecture. And do you know what the subject was?"

"Gorillas," I said, just to be smart.

She smirked. "Very good. Almost right. It was wild children. 'Feral children,' the sergeant called them. Kids that live in the forest—just babies sometimes they are, tossed out of home by their parents for one reason or another. Sometimes they look out for themselves, sometimes they are raised by animals—all sorts of animals: Wolves, apes, bears; one even lived with a herd of gazelle in Africa—but all these kids have one thing in common . . . they live by their senses. Supersenses. Like wild animals. Sight. Smell. Hearing. They can hear the tiniest sounds that normal humans can't. And all these senses work overtime, twenty-four hours a day. That's what the sergeant said. I don't think he'd lie, right?"

I nodded.

"Good. He says it's possible that we have a boy like this here in Jericho. And maybe over the years he's developed these animal senses, living in the bush with someone like Flannagan. And that's why no one can catch him. See? Because he's too smart for them."

I began to understand why Leena laughed at the welfare ladies, why she thought that nobody would ever catch Micky, but I didn't say that to Julia.

"So," she said, "just because our bed-wetting friend Keithy tells us that this boy ran far, far away when his sister was captured doesn't make it true. Oh no. We have no reason to believe this wild boy's a coward. *Au contraire,* as Ruby says. This wild boy could have been sitting in the Fergusons' cow shed taking photos of the event for all Keithy knew. Or of the people who captured her. Our father, for example. See, he mightn't even need to use his superpowers to find her. No. All he has to do is find the people who captured her. Easier still, the car that took her away. And how many cars like ours are there in Jericho . . . ?"

"One," I admitted.

"Quite right. One. Just ours. Parked in our drive every day and most nights . . . just when feral creatures like to prowl."

"You're saying that this kid comes in from way out at the Thumbs? About ten miles. That's silly . . ."

"How do you know that?" she asked.

"What?"

"That he comes in from the Thumbs?"

"I don't know. Not for sure. But Leena told me they lived in a cave out there, full of bats."

"That's where Bobby reckons they are too. The only place they could be, he says. I'll tell him that. But it doesn't make any difference to what I was saying. I think you've got the wrong idea. You're still confusing this kid with some invention of Keithy's. Kimmy, this is the twentieth century. This kid doesn't have to lope into town like some stray dog. He might get a lift. He might hop on the back of a truck. Some of those dairy boys are in and out as regular as clockwork . . . and all hours of the night too, if they have to do an early morning delivery down the coast. That's what Bobby thinks."

I was determined not to be afraid. "So," I said, "does

this mean he might be coming here? Is that what they're saying?"

"He might."

"Well it wouldn't do him any good. He couldn't get to Leena. Not with the bars."

"He doesn't know we've got bars, does he?"

She was right, but I couldn't admit it. "Go on," I said, trying to sound tough.

"Bobby thinks that we have to stop him. Not stop him because he's coming in for Leena—nobody could blame him for that—but because when he breaks his cover and comes out of that bush, he's an easy target. He can't run around Jericho like he does in the scrub . . . and the loonies know that. They're waiting."

"The loonies? What loonies?"

"Van Marseveen and Ward, for starters." She lowered her voice. "You remember that man Stafford, the dopey one at the inquest . . . the one that got the migraines? He killed himself. A week ago he overdosed on something. *Fini*. The end. People were saying that he was out after the boy to clear his name. Up at the site they're saying maybe he was guilty. And the other pair—Marseveen and Ward—they're getting blamed too. That's what Bobby heard. They reckon the only ones who can prove they're innocent are the Flannagan kids, but they can't get to them. They don't know that she's here, but they're on to the boy. They go up the hills on the weekend. They're going out to the farms following up sightings. Bobby says that they're idiots and couldn't track a herd of elephants, but if the kid's coming in closer, into town, they might get lucky . . ."

"He should warn the police. He shouldn't keep information like that to himself."

"He doesn't want to. Not with Ben Cullen there."

"But Ben Cullen *is* the police."

"He might be, but he's looking too. Bobby as good as told us that the time he found your fossils. It's just a game to Ben, he says. He's after a trophy—like hunting—like it's a wild animal he's after."

I couldn't listen to any more. "Tomorrow's Christmas. Can I go to sleep now?"

"I didn't mean to scare you, Kimmy . . . honest."

"Merry Christmas, Jules," I said, and slipped under the covers.

fifteen

after breakfast, when I was finally allowed into the living room, I saw straight away that there was no bike. I wasn't worried. Since it was the biggest present and the best, it would be brought in last. I waited, quite happy, watching everybody else opening theirs. But Julia wasn't so happy. Her first present was a hair dryer. She looked confused. She always dried her hair in the sun—or even in the wind through the Chevy window—the natural way, she said.

"It's for taking to school," my mother explained.

Then my father left the room and came back with a matched set of luggage. Again my mother thought she should explain. "I know that you asked for music, but you'll be needing cases for school, coming and going, you know."

So when Julia came to open my present to her, I was almost afraid to look. It was a monogrammed set of stationery made out of my best art paper; every sheet trimmed to size and individually decorated with her initials at the top.

"I made that myself," I said, "because . . ." I was going to say "because I want you to write to me from boarding school," but I could see that any more talk of school and her Christmas would be ruined.

I think that she understood. "Thanks, Kimmy," was all she said.

I opened the biggest present with my name on it first. It was a chemistry set.

"This is great," I said, lying my head off. "Really interesting." There were other things though; not what I would call "big" presents, but good: Some books, a mural called *The Pageant of History* to put on my bedroom wall and a model kit of the *Titanic* . . . but no bike.

Julia shoved her present into my hand. It was the best present I got that Christmas, even better than Pa's. She gave me a box of Lakeland coloring pencils, seventy-two of the most amazing colors: Aqua and magenta and vermilion and some with descriptive names like "forest green" and "regal purple" and "ice blue" and even colors that are not colors, such as copper and silver and gold.

"Where did you get these?" I said. "I've never seen anything like these."

"Of course not," she said with a smug look. "I ordered them out of your art catalog didn't I? The one Frank Tassel told me he'd given you."

I was surprised to hear that—the art catalog had been hidden in my drawer.

My parents were happy with their presents too. My father said that the leather bookmark with D'Arcy's embossed eagle was "very nice," and my mother didn't believe that I had done the fossil rubbings until I showed her my signature, sealed beneath the glass. She said they could hang on the wall in the reception room, which was exactly what I'd hoped she would say, and a compliment.

When we asked Leena to open some of her presents she didn't want to. She sat on the floor and hugged them to her but she wouldn't open them.

"No," she whispered to me, "I want to go last."

And she did. When everyone else had finished and the tree was surrounded by mountains of crumpled paper and strips of bright ribbon, she unwrapped her presents delicately, folding the paper neatly and stacking it beside her, "to look at later," she said.

She made me feel ashamed, sitting there waiting for her to hurry up so I could get my bike.

Finally, when she had her nightie and perfume and hair brush and a pile of new magazines that I bought for her and she had nodded and grinned at everybody, I thought, now someone will say "stay where you are," and my father will get up and bring in my bike. But instead my mother announced, "Well. That's the presents over for another year. Now, let's get this mess cleaned up so we can start thinking about lunch."

Julia looked at me. I shook my head.

"Mother," she said, "isn't there something else?"

"Something else?"

"Another present."

"Who for?"

"For Kimmy. A big one."

"A big what?" My mother was either a better actress than I thought or she had no idea what Julia was talking about.

Julia whispered something to her.

"A bike?" she said aloud. She turned to my father. "Ivan?"

"A mystery to me," he answered.

"You're teasing, aren't you . . ." I began.

Nobody responded.

I tried again. "It was delivered on Monday. I saw it next to the truck. It was silver and . . ."

My mother put her hand to her face.

"You signed for it," I reminded her, "I saw you."

"Oh dear," she muttered. "Oh dear . . . I signed for Julia's luggage . . . not that bike. The driver only took that out to get the luggage behind. The bike went out to the Fergusons'. It's for Keithy."

I felt my bottom lip quiver.

"Now, Kim," my father said, "you know how we feel about bikes."

I didn't cry, not in front of Leena—but I did when I got up to the eyrie.

Bobby arrived after lunch with presents for Julia and me. He gave her three cassettes—so she got her music after all—and he gave me a pocketknife. It didn't have as many functions as Pa's, but the handle looked like it was made of bone.

"Is that real?" I asked.

"It's made from the antler of a deer," he said, "and that's pretty real, isn't it?"

"But would they have killed the deer?"

"They might have."

"I wouldn't like it if they did," I said. "Deer are beautiful animals. They don't hurt anyone."

He laughed at me. "Nor do lambs. Nor do calves. But I bet you eat their meat."

I said I'd have to think about that.

It was a very hot day, so when Bobby had cleaned up the last of the lunchtime cake, he, Julia, and I went into the yard. A breeze was coming up from the Gate and we sat on the wall in the shade of my tree to talk for a while.

"Did your parents find out that I saw the girl?" Bobby asked.

"Well, I didn't tell them," Julia said, looking directly at me.

I couldn't be bothered saying anything.

"Where is she now?" he asked.

"In her room," Julia said. "Looking at magazines, I think."

He was quiet for a minute, then he said, "And when will she be going?"

That depended on the welfare people, I told him, and whether her brother turned up.

"But nobody's looking," he said. "Not officially, are they?"

I shrugged. I didn't know.

"Well," he said, "I didn't come over just because it's Christmas. I wanted to talk to your folks about going after those fossils. My dad says I can have the weekend after New Year off, if I want, so I have to know. It's just your dad . . ."

"Perfect timing," Julia said. "He's in the reception room, doing what he does worst."

At that moment my father was attempting to hang up the rubbings. As Julia said, there were certain things that my father could do and certain things that he definitely could not. I had seen him stitch a wound so neatly that a week later no one would have known that the skin had been broken. I had seen him remove a sliver of glass from an eyelid and the patient had not even blinked. But ask my father to turn a screw, tighten a bolt, or hammer a nail, and he was hopeless. Worse, he knew that he was, and blamed everybody else for it. So when Bobby said,

"No time like the present," and jumped down off the wall, I felt my stomach turn over.

"No," I protested. "He'll be in a bad mood."

Julia laughed. "What? A bad mood at Christmas? Our father? Never!" and she led Bobby around the house to the office. I followed.

My father was standing on a stepladder. He had a tack hammer in one hand and a nail in the other. His sleeves were rolled up; he was ready for work. My mother was supervising, holding up the first of the rubbings. Although it was clear that the operation had just begun, he was already grunting. She was soothing him, saying, "Now be careful. There's no hurry."

Bobby went over and said, "Can I give you a hand?"

My mother's face lit up at once, but my father looked down, scowling.

"There's no need," he muttered.

Bobby wasn't easily put off. "No trouble," he said, steadying the ladder with his boot. "Farm boys are used to fixing things."

My father ignored him. He lined up the nail and brought the hammer down—but there was no bang, only the muffled sound of metal against flesh.

"The trouble is," Bobby pointed out, "that your hammer's too small for your nail. You only need a tack for those pictures. And you're using—"

My father swung around ready to confront him, but my mother was faster. "Here," she said, holding out a jar of assorted nails to Bobby, "would any of these do?"

While my father examined his thumb, still scowling, Bobby sorted through the contents of the jar.

"How many are we wanting?" he said.

"Four," I volunteered.

"Four tacks we have. Now, Dr. M., if you'd come down, I could have this done in a minute."

They faced each other, Bobby holding the ladder, looking up; my father glaring at him.

"Ivan," my mother said, and he came down.

Bobby was up the ladder in a flash. "Here?" he asked, and drove the tack home. The first frame hung perfectly, and the next, and the next, until all four were in place. "There." He climbed down and stepped back. "How's that?"

"Wonderful," my mother said, but my father turned to go.

"Doctor," Bobby called. "Can I talk to you for a minute?"

I edged toward the corridor. Julia didn't move.

"Yes?" he said impatiently.

"Next weekend my dad has given me some time off. I was wondering if I might take Kimmy up the bush to collect a few more fossils . . . " He used the hammer to indicate those that now hung on the wall.

My father glanced down at his thumb, which must have been throbbing. "For how long?" he said, not looking up.

"Probably two days. We could camp out one night."

It's "no," I thought. For sure it's "no."

"'We'? Who is 'we'? Julia won't be—"

At the mention of her name, Julia came forward. "I don't want to go," she said. "I'm not spending my New Year tramping around in the bush. I already told Darling McMurtry that I was going to her place. She's having all the girls from my year over. It's the last chance we'll have to see each other, since we're all getting packed off to different schools. . . ."

I couldn't believe my ears. This was the biggest lie that I'd ever heard Julia tell—and I'd heard her tell some whoppers. Darling was a proper Townie and Julia *hated* her. She had never been to one of Darling's parties in her life.

My mother knew this as well as I did. "Julia . . ." she began, but our Jules was too fast.

"No, Mother," she said, "it's all settled. But it would be terrible if the boys weren't allowed to go. Look at those drawings Kimmy has done. I think they're wonderful. I never appreciated his talent. And now that he's got those artist's quality colored pencils that I gave him, it would be an awful waste if he didn't have the chance to use them to draw something worthwhile—like a mountain landscape. Don't you think?"

By the time she had finished, my father was looking hard at the rubbings, thinking.

"Ivan . . ." my mother said, getting ready to argue.

"It's quite all right, Helen," he broke in. "For once I agree with Julia."

Bobby nodded, but not without a glance at Julia, whose lie must have amazed him as much as it had my mother and me.

"Next weekend then," my father concluded and disappeared into his examining room, still nursing his thumb.

"There," Julia said, beaming in triumph. "I said it would be all right."

But my mother wasn't satisfied. "Julia," she said, "*is* there a party at Darling's that night?"

"Yes," Julia answered, obviously offended. "Bobby and Kim can drop me off. They'll be heading up that way . . . and they can bring me home too, the next day."

My mother's eyes narrowed. I doubted that she was convinced but she said, "Well, that's that then. Now, if we're going to have our Christmas dinner, we'd better get going."

I took Bobby up to my room to show him my presents. When we reached the landing, he stopped and said, "What do you reckon, Kimbo? Do you believe her?"

"Who?" I said, deciding it was best to play dumb.

"Julia. Do you believe what she said about going to Darling's?"

I was certain that she wasn't going to Darling's, but I wouldn't admit it. I said, "She'd better, or else . . ." I thought this sounded very deep and adult, and was pleased that I'd thought of it.

Bobby said nothing.

sixteen

Leena was quiet that afternoon. She did nothing but sit on the floor, folding and unfolding the sheets of Christmas wrapping kept from the morning. She refused to eat anything for dinner, though there was leftover turkey from lunch, and plenty of desserts, and even when I went in to show her some of the different colors in the Lakeland box, she didn't show any interest.

My parents weren't concerned at first, putting it down to the excitement of Christmas, but the next day, when she still hadn't spoken and had eaten almost nothing, they began to take her change in behavior more seriously.

"It might be shock," my mother told us. "A person might appear to manage a crisis very well, then collapse days later. Even weeks sometimes. But shock patients tend to have long sleeping spells, and Leena's not sleeping. So . . . I'm wondering if it's us. If we're all too much for her."

"I think you're all exaggerating," Julia said. "It's probably nothing. She had a good time at Christmas, and now she's depressed, that's all. I'll take in my new tapes and show her those new magazines and I bet she snaps out of it. I bet that I get her talking in five minutes."

She didn't. By midmorning Julia was back in my room, wanting to talk herself.

"She gets hold of that Christmas paper and unfolds it, then spreads it out on the floor and smooths it flat as if it was a hundred-dollar bill. The same with that new nightie. It's all folded up, and she holds on to it all the time. She won't let it out of her sight. And there's that brush, and the perfume. Every ten minutes she brushes her hair, then dabs some perfume on her neck, then she hides everything inside the nightie. Weird. I think she's getting ready to run away. She dabs on that perfume, she holds that nightie up against her, then she looks straight up at that window. You watch. She's thinking about getting out."

I did watch. That day and the day after, I tried to get Leena's attention. I worked on the alphabet project, I read stories, I drew pictures—but she wasn't interested. She didn't even look at me.

I didn't think Julia was right. If Leena had wanted to escape there wasn't anything stopping her. Her ankle was better. It was still bandaged, but she could walk on it if she wanted to.

The longer I watched Leena, the more I thought there was something else. She did the things that Julia said, that was true, but when she held the nightie it seemed to me that she was rocking. She cradled it in her arms and rocked, very gently, as if the nightie was a baby. Sometimes she would raise her hand and touch her cheek, running her fingers down toward her lips. Sometimes she would cry; not making any noise, but I saw tears. I thought that having her own things again might make her remember something, or some time when she had a mother and father and her life might not have been so terrible.

I thought about her brother, too, and what Julia had said on Christmas Eve: How he might love her and miss her, and how he might come in looking for her. I wondered if Leena thought the same. But I couldn't sit with her all the time, and when Julia told me that Bobby wanted to take me out to the farm to show me a surprise, I didn't think twice.

"Fine," I said. "I'll be in that."

As soon as we arrived we went over to the shed where Bobby did his machinery maintenance. I liked this shed; it was sometimes used as a barn, and the hay bales were stacked almost to the ceiling. Once, when Bobby and Julia had first started going together, I'd climbed all the way up to the top of the bales, but when I got there I could hardly breathe.

"Something stinks up here," I called, and sure enough, when Bobby shifted a few of the bales, he uncovered a dead kitten.

"It's one of our mouser's," he said. "She had five but a day or so later we only found four. We thought a snake must have got it, or a hawk."

"How did it die?" I wanted to know.

"Suffocated, I guess. Or starved. She must have brought the kittens up here, shifting them around like mother cats do, and it's dropped down and been trapped between the bales where she couldn't reach it."

But this day the shed was sweet with new hay. I could smell it as we crossed the yard.

"Have you got a calf in there?" I said, trying to be smart.

"A calf? Why would I put a calf in the shed?"

"I thought that might be the surprise."

He laughed. "No. It's more exciting than a calf."

I couldn't see anything that looked special—until he

pointed to a contraption laid out on the dirt floor. There were half a dozen fuel drums roped together on a wooden frame, and leaning against this was a rusty iron gate—a big fancy thing decorated with scrolls.

"That's it," he said. "How about that?"

I realized that this pile of rubbish was the surprise. "What is it?" I asked.

"A raft, Kimbo. What we use to cross the dam. Or that's what it's going to be, when I get this gate welded on. It's the platform that goes on top. And over that goes a piece of carpet—a kind of magic carpet, see?"

He kicked the gate with his boot and it crashed forward onto the wooden frame.

I stood there dumbfounded; then I heard Julia whisper, "Bobby, you have to tell him," and the beginnings of suspicion stirred in my brain.

"Tell me what?" I said, looking at Bobby.

"Well . . . We're going after the fossils, like we said, but while we're up there, I thought we might check on that Flannagan kid. Jules told me what his sister said, about them hiding in caves up at the Thumbs, and I'm betting he's still there. It's the only place he could be—I said that from the beginning. But if we walk in, or drive in like those other idiots, I reckon that kid would see us before we get a hundred yards. I reckon he sits up there on top of a rock and watches and laughs his head off. That's how come nobody's caught up with him. But if we go in by water—go around behind him, in the dark—then we'd be right there, nearly on top of him, before he even knew."

"Would you catch him?" I said.

"I couldn't catch him. I'd have to get help."

"What help? The police?"

"I might. That depends."

"On what?"

"On if he's there in the first place." Bobby didn't like too many questions. He was starting to get edgy.

"I'd be in trouble," I said. "I'm supposed to be collecting fossils. If my father knew we were looking for that boy, and about the raft . . ."

"You're frightened of Daddy, aren't you?" Julia sneered.

I was getting sick of her. "So are you," I said.

"Ooh!" she gasped, making a ridiculous pouting mouth. "And what's that supposed to mean?"

"I'm not stupid, that's what it means. I know that you're not going to Darling McMurtry's party. You're coming with us, aren't you? Tell the truth."

She didn't expect this. I saw her face color. "I *am* going to Darling's," she said. "Bobby will drop me off at her gate, I'll go in, I'll say 'Happy New Year,' then I'll leave. Easy." She folded her arms after saying this, which was a childish way of claiming victory, I thought.

But she'd reckoned without Bobby. "Jules," he said, "I'm not doing that."

She turned to face him, ready to fight. "Why not? It's not a lie. Not like he said."

"It's not the truth either, and I don't want to do it. If your folks found out that I spent the night with you, there'd be big trouble."

She curled her lip at him then, which was a mistake.

"Kimbo," he said, "I felt sorry for you, always stuck in that house. I'd suffocate, I would. That's why I thought you'd like to get out. Have an adventure, like the kids in your books. Tom Sawyer or someone. Geez, when I was a kid, I was always up to something; off somewhere by myself. Up in the caves, out pig shooting. But, if you don't want to go, well . . ."

"I do want to go," I insisted. "And I'm not scared. You don't want to listen to Julia all the time."

He laughed and Julia walked away.

"Okay," he said, "we'd better leave her out of this, I reckon. She's had enough for one day. Now, are you going, for sure?"

"Yes," I said.

"Okay, let's get on with it. I'll show you a plan. Here . . ." and without bothering to look at Julia, who was still standing at the door with a face like thunder, he dropped to his knees and started drawing a map in the dirt. "Now," he said, "let's say that this here's the old loggers' road. I'll take the raft down and leave it there the day before. And after that . . ."

The drive home that afternoon was pretty miserable. Julia said nothing, and it wasn't because Bobby ignored her. All the way he cracked jokes and tried to get her to talk, but it was a waste of time.

Although my father had told me not to, I wound the window down and put my arm out to brush the ferns with my fingertips.

seventeen

I had nothing to do with the preparations for my trip with Bobby; he worked out everything with my mother. I'd say that she phoned him at least six times, asking him questions about what I should take. On the one chance I had to speak to him I said, "But what about if we find some fossils; what will I collect them in?"

I heard him laughing. "What if we find some fossils? We'll find some fossils all right, I guarantee. Tell you what; you get some cotton wool off your mom. That would be really good to pack them in. It won't take up room in your backpack, and you can use it as you need it. Okay?"

That was my contribution to the trip: Cotton wool.

When the day came Bobby drove the Chevy into the yard. This was the first time he had done that. Usually, if he was picking up Julia, he would park in the side lane or behind the garage, but always outside the wall. Not this time. This time he drove straight in.

I was in my room, all packed, but wondering if I could stuff another jacket in, when I heard him arrive.

Julia must have heard him too. She came to my door. "Are you ready?" she said.

"I've been ready since yesterday," I answered.

She made a face as if to say, *Well, aren't you good?* but I added, "Mom did everything. It wasn't me."

"Naturally," she said.

I ignored her.

Julia didn't forgive and she never forgot. She hadn't spoken to Bobby since that afternoon up at his farm. But he wasn't the only reason that she was angry. Ruby Parsons had phoned offering her work at the Empire over New Year. The phone in the reception room had been unattended and the call went through to my father's examining room. Normally he wouldn't have picked it up, but this time he had no choice. The answer he gave Ruby was no. Julia was going to a friend's party.

Julia didn't hear of this from my father; she heard it from Ruby herself when they happened to meet in the street. There was a terrible to-do that night.

The circumstances were made worse by Leena. She wouldn't eat while any of us were in the room, but if we took in a tray and left it, when we came back something would be gone, like a piece of fruit or a cup of tea half-drunk. Apart from this, she seemed to have lost all interest in anything except her presents. She still kept the perfume, the brush, the nightie, and the wrapping paper right beside her.

The one time my mother tried to put the nightie away, Leena let out such a terrible howl that I came down to find out what was going on. She was left hugging the thing, grubby as it was from all her handling.

"We can't keep this up," was all my mother said.

This was the situation on the morning Bobby came to take me out. I picked up my bags and squeezed past Julia, who blocked my door. If what she had said to me was supposed to be good-bye then I wasn't going to be bothered with her. But I did go to see Leena.

I opened the door and found her in the corner, staring up at the window. The nightie was on the floor beside her. She had one hand on it, as if it was going to be stolen or vanish at any moment.

I said, "Leena, I came to say good-bye. Bobby's taking me up to the North Arm for a couple of days."

She didn't reply but I knew she'd heard.

"We're going after some of those fossils, like the ones I drew. You remember, don't you?"

"Yes," she answered.

This was the first word that I'd heard from her for days.

"Would you like me to bring you one back?" I said.

"Yes," she said again.

I couldn't wait any longer and went to the door. "See you," I said.

She turned around completely and called, "Micky's up there."

"Where?" I said, playing dumb.

"I told you."

I shook my head. "I can't remember."

"With the bats," she whispered. "That's where he is."

There was no one else to hear, and that was how she wanted it I supposed.

Bobby was waiting in the kitchen with my mother. She'd already given him the food.

"Your mom thinks that we're going for a month, Kimbo," he said, indicating the size of the carton at his feet.

"Maybe she thinks we're going to meet up with some other party," I joked, but nobody laughed.

When the Chevy was packed, my father came out and said something to Bobby which I couldn't hear. I saw him nod a few times and supposed that he was getting last-minute instructions on how to care for me. I wondered what my father would know about camping that would be of any use.

Julia appeared too. She leaned against the kitchen door and folded her arms, still behaving like a child. Bobby finished with my father and went straight over to her, but she walked off, disappearing into the house. I felt sorry for him, although he took it pretty well.

"Ready when you are," he said.

I shook hands with my father then turned to hug my mother. She stopped me and held me at arm's length.

"Wait," she said, and started removing the upside-down nurse's watch from her uniform, adding mysteriously, "you never know when you might need this." She pinned it onto my shirt, where it dangled like a toy medal, then kissed me a hundred times.

Bobby finally got me into the Chevy. I sat in the front seat, which was a big deal, since I hadn't been there before on account of Julia. I waved as we drove out of the yard.

That was when I saw Leena—or thought that I did— at the downstairs window, peering out from behind the bars.

I began firing questions at Bobby from the moment we drove away. First, I wanted to know what my father had said to him.

"He told me that I had to make sure you brush your teeth," he said, stony faced.

I didn't believe this, but not getting any better answer I pressed on: What if it rained? Had he taken the raft up?

Did it float? What if the stove wouldn't light? What if . . . until finally he took both his hands off the wheel and held them up in front of him: "Please," he said, looking up to heaven. "If there's anyone up there, make this kid shut up!"

I reminded him that this trip had been his idea.

"That's true," he said. "Okay, you can ask me any questions you like for the next two days and I guarantee that I'll answer them."

"Good," I said, "because there'll be a lot. But right now I've got something to tell you," and I repeated for him what Leena had said about her brother as I left.

"I told you so," he said. "Right from the beginning, I guessed they'd be up in the Thumbs."

"But why didn't you tell?"

He laughed. "Why should I tell? If I'd had half a chance, I'd have been up there with them."

We left the main road at a point just past the turnoff to Pa's place.

"We could stop and see old Cossey if you like," Bobby said, but I didn't want to.

The track was rough and narrow, threading through eucalypt forest, but it was used—mostly by duck shooters, Bobby said—and although the Chevy rolled and bumped, he didn't slow down. Then the dam suddenly appeared through a gap in the trees, shining silvery blue like the picture on the lid of my Lakeland pencil box.

For a half mile or more the track followed the shoreline. In places where there had once been gullies, swampy backwaters had formed, filled with gray masses of dead scrub, but dotted here and there with clumps of water reeds. The tires of the Chevy squelched in the ooze.

"There's probably as much water under us as there is in the dam itself," Bobby said. "The entire North Arm is waterlogged. All of this vegetation will die. You wait and see what's happened in the big timber."

When the track petered out into reedy pools, Bobby ran the Chevy into the scrub and stopped.

"The end of the line," he said. "The fossils are that-a-way. We hoof it from here."

"How far?" I asked. I couldn't get any clear sense of direction.

"About another half mile."

It was ten o'clock by my mother's upside-down watch. "How long will it take?" I said.

"Maybe half an hour. It's a bit of a climb and it's rough. We'll leave everything in the car. All you'll need is your backpack."

The ground rose almost immediately. I guessed that we were climbing a ridge that formed part of the foothills of the Thumbs. Sure enough, just when I thought I would have to ask him to slow down, Bobby stopped and called, "There, Kimbo. See? To the right."

The three gray peaks of the Thumbs now loomed above the bush, like a scene from *The Lost World*. If a pterodactyl had lifted from among them, beating its leathery wings, I would not have been surprised.

"Go on," Bobby said. "Go up a bit higher and tell me what you can see."

I did as I was told, then looked back. The view had changed. In the shadow of the larger mountains, there seemed to be another. "There's a fourth one," I said. "A little one hidden behind."

"You don't say," he laughed.

"But, I've seen the Thumbs," I protested. "If I climb up to my eyrie . . ."

"That's the trouble with you Townies. You only see the view from one side. But you wait, we're going right round there later, through the tall timber, and then you'll see. That's the wild side, Kimmy, believe me."

The fossil bed was at the bottom of the ridge, in the bank of a creek that ran into the dam. With all the rain the previous spring, the banks had given way and a dark band of brittle stone had been exposed.

"See how the different layers have formed," Bobby said, kneeling to show me. "But the shells are only in one. Here."

He prized a stone loose, wiping it clean on his jeans. It was crowded with shells, one pressed over another, the same as the pieces I had used for my rubbings.

I reached out and loosened a lump. It came away easily, and without even cleaning it I could see what I had found. "There must be millions," I said, looking along the bank.

"Probably," he agreed. "Depends on how deep the layer goes back into the bank. See, the shellfish must have been thick on the seabed, feeding maybe, when this mud slide came down and covered them. There must be other things too; all sorts of sea creatures."

He left me then and walked farther up the creek, looking for signs of more, I supposed.

I took off my backpack and busied myself collecting what I could, freeing the stones from the clay with my fingers.

When Bobby came back and saw what I had collected, he shook his head. "Kimbo, you should only take what you can carry. Leave the rest. You can come back another day. Or somebody else might. Some expert, see? Some scientist, maybe. I tell you what," he said, squatting down, "we'll make two piles. We'll put those that show a lot of shells in one pile, and leave the rest for someone else."

"Sure," I said, "but what about the other sort?"

"What other sort?"

"The sort that aren't shells." I took a piece of stone from my shirt pocket and held it out to him.

He looked at it. "I told you there'd be something else here. Do you know what this is?"

"A crayfish." I wasn't stupid.

"It sure as hell is. It's a freshwater cray. Just a baby. I haven't seen one since I was a kid, and here's you pulling one out of a clay bank a million years old. Is it the only one?"

"So far. It came out with a big piece but it broke off. There might be more."

He turned a stone in his fingers. "Maybe we'd better leave this for now, Kimbo. Take what we've got and get out of here. We don't really know what we're doing, do we? Maybe we should do what I said. Take this stuff in and show it to the experts."

"What experts? I'm not handing them over to Mrs. Pullar and the Historical Society."

He thought for a minute. "How about we take them somewhere else? Maybe we could get them down the coast some time, to the university, where they could be properly studied. You know, understood."

When we had made a pile of the "definites," I took the cotton wool out of my bag and we packed the stones so they could be carried without damage.

We left the rest behind and walked back to the car. I checked the time—it was nearly two o'clock—and asked how long it would take to go around to the raft.

"Not so long," he said. "The way I go, up through the big timber, we give the Thumbs a pretty wide berth before we come back in. I'd say we'd be there in an hour. But I don't want to be on the water until dusk. If that boy's up there hanging about, I don't want to be seen. That's the whole idea of coming around from behind."

I hadn't given a thought to the boy. I said, "Do you think that he's in there? Watching us?"

"Who'd know? Sound carries out here. If he's there, he could've heard the car already. He might even have seen us at the fossil bank. But he might be anywhere."

A shiver ran down my spine.

"Hey," he said, "we don't have to go up there. We've got the fossils. That's what we really came for. And they're beauties too. We can go home if you like. I can come back another time and look for that kid. I don't want you getting—"

"I want to keep going," I said.

"All right. I say we leave here now and eat when we get to the raft. If it's the boy we're looking for, we'll be waiting around over there until dark, anyway."

We drove back to the main road and headed north. At first I could see the Thumbs, then they disappeared behind the canopy of the forest and the road seemed to be crushed between the trees that crowded right to its edge. But when Bobby turned off again I was taken by surprise. There was a track, but it was nowhere near as clear as the one down to the fossils.

"Who made this?" I asked, as the Chevy bucked from rut to rut.

"This is the old loggers' road. A timber company used to have a contract to cut cedar here, but that's long gone. It's hardly used now, except by the odd forestry ranger. It was a proper mongrel getting the Chevy down with the raft on top, I can tell you."

I guessed that we were approaching the dam as the trees began to thin out. Dead trunks were everywhere, still standing, but bleached the color of old bones.

"It's the dam seepage that kills them," he said. "They don't have to go under to die. The soil's so waterlogged they drown standing up."

We cleared the trees and stopped at an inlet dotted with islands. They were no bigger than our yard, but each was covered with dead timber, the same bone white trunks that I had seen at the edge of the forest.

"See," Bobby said, "all drowned. Those islands would have been the tops of hills once. But that's progress . . . and anyhow, the ducks think they're great."

We left the car and went down to the water. The raft was there, safe and sound, hidden among the reeds. It seemed little different from when I last saw it, except that the gate had been welded to the fuel drums to form a platform, and a piece of carpet—magic carpet, Bobby had called it—was thrown over that. A pole about three yards long was lying on top.

"Will it float?" I asked.

To answer me, Bobby began pushing it into the water. "Come on. There's only one way to satisfy doubters."

I pushed as hard as I could, until suddenly I felt the weight go and it floated free.

"There," he said, standing back. "No problems. But be warned, when we get on, it'll settle a bit." He reached out with the pole and hauled it back to shore. "So, what's our Kimbo most scared of now: A watery grave or the wild boy of Jericho?"

I made a face and he laughed, putting his arm around my shoulders and leading me back to the car. "Don't worry. She's not going to go down. But as for that boy, well . . . I don't know . . . He might jump out any time. . . ." And before I knew what was happening he was on top of me, tickling me.

It was after three o'clock before we had anything to eat. We went through the food supplies and decided that some ham sandwiches must have been for our lunch, and polished those off. Then we discovered some apple charlotte and ate that too. I was never a big eater—my mother said that I only nibbled, like a mouse—but I ate everything that day. There were two cartons of juice; two thermos flasks, one of soup and one of tea; a packet of biscuits; a string of sausages; and some rolls.

"Where's our breakfast then?" Bobby wanted to know. "I don't see any cereal in here. Or bacon."

I said maybe that was my mother's way of getting us to come home early.

"Probably," he agreed, "but I'm not a pretty sight without a good brekky, I warn you."

When he had finished eating, he put his hands behind his head and lay back on the grass. "This is the life," he said. "Getting out like this. When I was a kid, before I got involved in the farm, I used to come down here all the time. It was thick bush then. There was a creek down there . . ." he pointed the toe of his boot in the direction of the raft, ". . . where I used to catch those freshwater crays and take them home for mom to cook."

"Didn't she worry?" I said. "My parents won't let me out of their sight, unless I'm with Jules."

"Not mine. There were nine of us. Nobody would even know if I was missing. It's different now that I'm the only one left. I have to ask every time I want to go out. People say, 'Oh, it must be just wonderful to be out on the farm. All that fresh air. Growing things and looking after the animals. . . .' Unless they've been there, they wouldn't know. Farms can be a worse trap than a nine-to-five job, I reckon. You have to be up to milk at four every morning, rain or shine, summer and winter. If you do go anywhere, you have to be back by afternoon to start all over again."

"I thought you loved the farm," I said.

He laughed. "Pretty soon, my parents are going to sell up and move down to the coast. My mom was a city girl, but my dad was raised on that farm. You know, he never even saw the sea until he was thirty-five, and that was on his honeymoon when Mom made him go. They've both had a gutful of cows. And when they go, I'll go too."

I couldn't believe my ears. "What will you do for a job?" I said. "You didn't finish school."

"I'll go back. I'll study science. I'll find out why all those snails died. And what went down with them, like that crayfish, and how come those mountains got pushed up there. That's what I want to know."

"But you can't just study. You would have to earn some money, wouldn't you?"

"Kimbo, I'll have money. When my folks sell that farm, they'll make a fortune. Some smart developer from the coast will snap it up and divide it into building lots. 'Jericho Glades Estate: Lake and mountain views.' That's the way it's going to be, Kimbo."

"Does Julia know that?"

He turned to look at me. "Why?" he said.

I shrugged. "I just wondered, that's all."

He shook his head. "No, Jules doesn't know. And I haven't been game to tell her."

Neither of us spoke after that.

Just before six we loaded the raft and Bobby pushed off. I sat on the carpet covering the gate and cradled my backpack in my arms. There was no noise, except for the lapping of the water beneath us and the occasional cry of a wood duck from the islands. I stared around. I wondered which pencil I would use to color those dead trees: Deathly white; silver ghost; tombstone gray . . . but the light of the setting sun was like magic, and nothing stayed the same long enough for me to choose.

When we came out of the inlet onto the open water, Bobby whispered, "There," and pointed over my shoulder. The view had changed again. The Thumbs reared from the scrub, dark and menacing, like creatures from a primeval sea. The three larger peaks were now behind, and before us stood the fourth.

"It looks different," I said. "Not as wild as the others."

He grinned. "You'll see. It's got a character all of its own . . . it's a bit like you, hey Kimbo?"

As the last of the sun died away, we entered an inlet surrounded by hundreds of fallen logs. The silvered trunks lay one on top of the other in terrible confusion, right to the water's edge.

"A deadfall," Bobby whispered. "Years ago a landslide flattened the forest. It's another reason no one comes in from this side."

We beached the raft at an opening in the logs and carried our things onto the land. Bobby was faster than me over the fallen timber. He seemed to have a way of running low, leaping from log to log, as if he was born to it. I went over on all fours, terrified that I would slip and fall down into the darkness beneath.

When I caught up with him he had already chosen a site for our camp. We were surrounded on three sides by the deadfall, but the fourth opened out toward the Thumbs.

"Do you really want to use the tent?" he asked. "That deadfall's a natural barrier, and it's a nice clear night. What do you think?"

I nodded, though I didn't understand his reasoning. I had no fear of anything that might come out of the water; it was what lurked in the mountains that frightened me.

"Can we have dinner?" I asked. "There's plenty of wood here for a good fire."

Bobby looked at me as if I was crazy. "If we can't talk out loud, we can't have a fire, can we? If you lit a fire here, he would see it from miles away."

"Why did we bring a lamp then?"

"Just in case."

The problem of dinner remained. I had seen a string of sausages, and knew for certain they were raw. "So," I said, "how do we cook the sausages?"

"Kimbo, you're asking an awful lot of questions. Just remember, you're the one who agreed to look for this kid—and going without is the price you have to pay. There's hot soup in the flask, and bread rolls and biscuits."

"I like soup," I said. I didn't want him getting into a huff, like my father.

After we'd eaten he disappeared behind the logs to have a pee. I did the same—a bit like a dog, I thought—but when I came back, he was already in his sleeping bag, lying with his hands beneath his head as he had by the inlet that afternoon.

"Is it time for bed?" I asked.

"Nothing much else to do," he said. "Not until light."

"Should I get changed?" I didn't want to break any camping rules.

"Nope. Just drop your shorts, that's all. But keep your underwear on . . . and keep your shorts next to you, see," his jeans were in a heap beside him, "within reaching distance . . . just in case."

It was the second time he'd said that. "In case of what?" I said.

"In case there's an emergency."

"What sort of emergency?"

He groaned. "How about an attack of vampire bats!"

I took this as a signal to be quiet and stared up at the stars. But after awhile I said, "Honest, what did my father tell you this morning? I don't believe it was about making me brush my teeth."

"He told me to drown you as soon as I got the chance."

"Honest," I reminded him.

"Honest? What say you don't like 'honest'?"

"I just want the truth," I insisted.

"Okay. He said, 'Remember, he's just a child.'"

"What did he mean by that?"

"Buggered if I know. But I decided it meant that we should have a good time—like I did when I was a kid."

I said that sounded fine and that he could start by telling me how to catch crayfish and about the loggers, and after that . . .

He groaned again. If I wanted answers, he said, I had to ask questions one at a time. I did, until I stopped having to ask at all. He talked on and on about the old days: The gold, the big timber, the mountains and the wild men that lived in them. As I listened I drifted away, my dreaming thick with stars.

I woke up to Bobby shaking me. "Kimmy," he was saying, "Kimmy . . ."

I sat up, groggy with sleep. It was still night.

"Are you listening?" he said, and when I nodded he spoke with an urgency that frightened me. "Something's happening up on the mountain. I heard a hare scream, and now there's a fire, see?"

He took my head in his hands and turned it toward the fourth peak. At first I could see nothing and tried to pull away, but then I saw: Light flickered in the rocks about halfway up; not bright and steady like an electric light, but dim and ghostly, flaring and fading.

". . . I reckon it's our boy," he whispered, releasing me. "Are you coming to find out?"

I looked at the time. "It's after midnight," I mumbled, but this was the only protest I could manage. Bobby was already fully dressed and I was afraid that he would go without me.

I got up and dressed myself. As I tied my shoes I said, "How can you be sure that it's him?"

"Because it makes sense. I didn't say so before—I didn't want to stir you up—this fourth Thumb, it doesn't look much, not from the outside, but it's the one with the caves. Deeper than you could imagine, going right down into the earth. That's what Leena told you, see? Where he hides. He hunts at night, doesn't he, and by day he lives there, with the bats." He turned and looked toward the shimmering light.

"What will happen if we find him?"

He sighed and shook his head. "I don't know. But I'm sure of one thing. Something terrible happened to those kids. Something so terrible that they ran away rather than face it. But they know. Your Leena knows, and this boy, and one other."

"The murderer?" I said.

"Yes, that's the one."

The gooseflesh prickled on my neck.

As soon as we were clear of the deadfall the ground began to rise, and in no time we were following a gully that led directly into the rocks. My soft-soled shoes weren't made for this sort of walking and Bobby was constantly having to wait for me to catch up. It was easier for him, wearing boots.

Once, when I thought that I had lost him, I turned a corner and there he was, sitting on a rock. He pointed to a clump of stunted trees sprouting from a ledge above us. "See them," he said. "They should be huge—they're those giant figs—but they haven't grown a bit since I was a kid. There's no nourishment for vegetation up here."

"How much farther?" I wasn't interested in the wonders of nature.

"There's a bit of a climb, then it drops away into a ravine. There's grass down there. It's a good place to trap hares, and that's what he's been doing, I guarantee. But you get into the caves from up here—so from now on no more talk. And be careful of the rocks—set one rolling and he'll hear it for sure. You ready?"

He didn't wait for an answer.

Minutes later I almost walked into him, stopped slap-bang in the middle of the track. He put a hand out, telling me to be quiet. I looked around him. Before us the track opened into a saucer-shaped depression, perhaps ten or twelve yards across, and on the far side of this I saw the flicker of firelight among a tumble of rocks.

He put his mouth to my ear, whispering, "I'm taking a look. Wait." Then he disappeared.

I pressed myself flat against the rocks. I felt my knees go weak and was afraid that they would buckle under me.

Suddenly Bobby was back. Without a word he grabbed my arm and pulled me down the track after him. He stopped beneath the stunted figs. "Sorry Kimbo, but I wanted to get you away. Somewhere in the rock above that clearing there's a cave. I couldn't see an entrance, not in the dark, but that's where the fire is. And whoever's in there is cooking meat. Can you smell it?"

I nodded.

"It must be him. I say we wait here until morning. Soon as it's light, we take a look."

I thought he was crazy. "In daylight?" I said. "I'm not going up there in daylight."

"No. You're wrong. He'll be asleep by then, I bet. That's why they can't get him. In the day he stays in and sleeps. See?"

"If we see him, then we can go, can't we?" I said, and added in case he misunderstood. "You wouldn't try to catch him, would you?"

He twisted his head to read the face of my mother's watch. "It's nearly three." He slipped his jacket off and folded it. "Here, put your head down on this for an hour or so. Don't worry, you'll be all right."

I leaned against the rock and looked up at the night sky. The gnarled branches of the figs were silhouetted above me. I thought of my own tree arching over the wall at home. I thought of the trees that had hidden the Yarama, the vampire thing that terrified Queenie.

The sky was pale gray when I woke up and the bats were flying in off the water.

"You see," Bobby said, "they're coming home for the day."

I rubbed my eyes. My head felt dizzy.

"I nodded off for a while too," Bobby said. "I could do with a drink."

"Couldn't we just go home?" I suggested.

He roughed up my hair. "I'm going on, but you can wait here if you want."

"No," I said. "I'll be all right. Just let me have a pee."

I went behind the rocks. He was getting sick of me, I could tell, but my neck was sore and I was hot and giddy.

When I came back he saw my hangdog face. "Hey," he said, "I've been a bit hard on you, haven't I?"

I shrugged. "I'm just a child, remember." I meant

this as a joke, but I think he took it the wrong way.

We climbed the track for the second time. At the point where it opened into the clearing, Bobby stopped and looked up. He was watching the home-coming bats. They seemed to swoop from the sky directly above us, hover uncertainly, then vanish into the face of the rock.

Bobby turned to me and pointed. "There," he whispered.

We circled the clearing under cover of the rocks. All the while I kept my eye on the spot where the bats had disappeared. I knew one thing: If they could fly in, something else could come out.

When we had completed our circuit, Bobby watched the bats at closer range. They vanished beneath a ledge about five yards away. One of the fig trees sprouted from the rocks, and somewhere among its roots, deep in the dark shadow of the ledge, was the entrance to a cave.

With one signal only—a finger to his lips—Bobby dropped to his knees and crawled even closer. At the clump of roots he stretched up into the dark. A bat beating down struck him hard on the back; others veered away suddenly to circle the clearing. Then he was gone.

The fear that had come over me the night before began to return. The same dryness in my mouth; the same weakness in my knees. Even though it was almost day, I was shivering. I said to myself, over and over, "Stop it, stupid. Stop it . . . "

I was still saying this as I pulled myself up into the clump of roots. The opening to the cave appeared right in front of me: A yawning black hole, splotched white all over with the droppings of bats. I had to go in, that was all there was to it.

At first there was a dark tunnel, pitch black and terrible, but it widened, and a sickly gray light penetrated, growing brighter and brighter the farther I went. I must have crawled twenty yards before I was able to get to my feet and reach up to touch the roof.

The tunnel ended in what seemed to be full daylight. I guessed that this had been a proper cave, and much longer, but years before the roof must have fallen in and now the sun broke through, at least in places.

I saw Bobby when I reached the light. He was standing at the edge of what looked like a well. Here the floor of the cave must have collapsed at the same time as the roof, leaving a hole that seemed to be bottomless. Bats flitted in the void, and from far above, on the surface I supposed, the roots of trees fell all the way down—how far, I couldn't tell—like the bell ropes in *The Hunchback of Notre Dame*.

A narrow ledge ran partway around the perimeter. Bobby was standing on the far side of this, beckoning to me.

I looked at the width of the ledge that I was supposed to go around. I was feeling worse—feverish and lightheaded—but I went on, pressing against the wall.

When I reached him, he pointed down.

The wall was full of caves running deep into the rock. Bats roosted everywhere, but there, on a jutting ledge opposite us, I saw a sight that I will never forget.

A knotted root as thick as my arm hung down in front, and judging from the position of the knots, I could see it was used as a ladder. I saw a fireplace with a roasting spit, some pots and pans, a tattered suitcase, and against the far wall, asleep on a pile of rags or blankets, I saw a boy. Micky, I was certain.

I think it was at that time that Bobby realized I was sick. I can't say exactly what happened, but I know that I started to sway, and if he hadn't grabbed me and held me, I would have fallen headfirst into the pit.

I know that Bobby half carried, half dragged me along the tunnel and down the track to the camp. I know that he punted me back to the Chevy and got me out along the forest road. All of these things I remember. But there is one thing that I remember more clearly than most.

As we reached the beginning of the tunnel, Bobby left me. My head was spinning and my vision was blurred, I know, but I saw him do this very clearly. He leaned over the pit, and when he straightened up I saw that he had pulled in the knotted root which was the boy's ladder. He rolled it in a pile on the floor of the tunnel, like an electrician rolls a cable. I was very hazy about most other things, but I saw Bobby do that—and I knew, even then, that he had trapped my wild boy forever.

eighteen

Just as we cleared the forest road and came onto the asphalt, I vomited in the Chevy. Bobby pulled over to see how I was, but I guess one look was enough.

"I'm dropping you off at Pa Cossey's," he said. "He'll look after you. I've got things to do."

The next thing I knew I was sitting in Pa's kitchen with a bucket between my legs, heaving my heart out.

In the background, I heard Bobby talking on the phone, and then the Chevy started up and drove away.

When I couldn't be sick any more, Pa took the bucket and sat beside me. He asked me if I was feeling better.

"Yes, thanks," I croaked, "but I'm still giddy."

He handed me a glass of water. "You looked terrible," he said. "White as a ghost."

I didn't care. I just wanted to go home. "Did Bobby ring my father?" I asked.

"He was out on a call. Your mom said she'd send him over as soon as he came home."

I knew that could be a long time and I didn't want to be cooped up with Pa, having to talk. "I feel awful," I said. "Could I sit outside?"

He helped me out to an old cane lounge chair that stood in the shade of his candlenut tree. Way off, across the dam, I could see the Thumbs glinting in the sun.

"You two were up there, hey?" he said, sitting beside me.

"Yes," I said, "but I got sick and mucked it up."

He was looking at me very hard, I could tell. "Did you walk through the bush?" he said.

I didn't feel like talking, so I nodded and hoped he would leave me alone.

He changed his position and put his arm along the back of the chair. I moved away, but he reached out again, and this time his hand touched my hair.

"Don't, Pa," I said. I tried to get up, but I was too weak and, before I could stop him, his fingers pressed against my neck—at a spot behind my ear—and I yelped with pain.

He took his hand away. "You've got a tick, son," he said. "That's what's wrong with you."

I put my hand where his had been. I felt a sort of lump there, like a mole or a wart, that hurt like crazy. I moved my fingers higher, and brushed against another, and another, in my hair.

"My head's full of them," I whispered.

He looked where I showed him, rubbing my hair the wrong way to see better. He made clucking noises in his throat. "Big ones, too," he said. "All full of blood."

When he was satisfied that he'd found them all, he said, "They have to come out. I can do it if you like."

"Can't I wait for my father?" I said. I was frightened of the pain.

"You could, but he might be awhile. And every minute they're in there, they're burrowing in deeper."

"Would it hurt?"

"Not the way I do it."

His voice had a strange tone that made me look at him.

He raised his eyebrows. "What's the matter?"

"Who else have you taken them out of?" I asked.

"Other children," he said.

I thought that he was making this up. He had been coming to our place for years. I knew there were no other children. I leaned forward to avoid his touch and as I did, I noticed his boots. A rush of memories flooded my brain: The sound of boots on gravel; Pa staring up at a barred window; his questions about Leena; and her crouching inside, muttering, "Mister, Mister . . ."

I pulled myself up and stumbled forward, vomiting against the trunk of the candlenut tree.

"Come on," he said. "Let me help you. . . ."

I felt his hand touch me and spun around, shouting, "Get away. You're the killer, aren't you? You're Mister. . . ."

My knees folded and I dropped to the ground. His boots were right in front of me. I was sick again.

When I looked up he had backed away. I wiped my mouth with the back of my hand.

"What did I kill?" was all he said.

I couldn't understand how he could ask me that. I edged away toward the tree.

"Well?" he said. "Tell me."

"Flannagan." I spat the name at him.

"Me?" he said. "Me?" and then he started laughing. "Why would I kill Flannagan?"

"I don't know," I muttered, "but you did. I know you did."

I estimated my chances of making it to the phone, but before I could move, he said, "You found him, didn't you?"

"Who?"

"Micky, that's who."

I didn't answer.

"This is the silliest conversation I've ever heard," he said. "Let me get you inside."

He started to walk toward me, and I backed away, holding the tree for support.

"What the hell is wrong with you?" he yelled.

I kept the tree between us. I wanted him to know how I found him out. "I saw you looking up at Leena's window, asking all those questions. And she knew that you were there too. She heard your boots crunching on the gravel . . . just waiting to go in after her."

"No, no, no," he said. "You've got it all wrong. I wouldn't hurt her. It was me who kept her alive. Right here. You can ask her if you want. You ask her about my tree." He pointed to the candlenuts above me. "That's what they came here for, her and Micky. I caught them raiding that tree, after the nuts. He was up there like a monkey, chucking them down to her. . . ."

I felt my knees going, but didn't dare sit down. I gripped the tree tighter.

"They came here twice a week. I started leaving the fruit out, to make it easier. They knew that I was here, but they had me summed up. I wasn't any threat. I started sitting on the back steps, just to watch, and then I came out here. That's when I got to know them. They came right up. Her first, and then him, Micky. . . ."

"Why didn't you say? Why didn't you tell someone?"

"When I heard that she was taken away, to some orphanage, I thought, why should I let them have him? Why should I let them put him behind bars? Poor little kid. If they lock him up it'll kill him. Believe me, he's not like her. He's a proper wild one, that Micky."

"They haven't got him yet," I said.

"No, they haven't, have they?" His face lit up like only Pa's could; like it did when he gave me a present. I knew then that I was wrong.

"Sorry, Pa," I mumbled, but before I could explain I started crying my head off like a stupid baby.

"Come on," he said. "I'll have a look at those ticks."

He took me into the house and left me sitting at the kitchen table. In a minute or two he reappeared with a bottle of kerosene, some antiseptic, some cotton wool, a bowl of boiling water, and a pair of tweezers.

"Now I'm not pretending that this is medically correct," he said, "but it's quick and painless and it gets rid of the suckers. Are you ready?"

First he doused a swab of the cotton wool in the kerosene, then he dabbed this on one of the ticks. I felt a sting in my neck, and tried to pull away, but before I could, Pa had the tweezers on it and tugged. The next second he held out to me a thing that looked like a raisin, except that it had legs and wriggled.

"One," he said, and dropped it, still wriggling, into the boiling water.

When they were all out, he got me to lie down on his sofa and brought me a mug of tea. "That's full of sugar," he said, "to get your energy back. Drink it all down and you'll feel better."

I propped myself up on the cushions and sipped the tea while he cleared the "operating table," as he called it. Then he sat beside me.

"So," he said, "how do you feel?"

"A bit better," I admitted. "It must be the tea."

"Ma always said I could make a good cuppa—but I tell you, those Flannagan kids never stayed for one, not after I pulled out their ticks."

"They were the other children, weren't they?" I said.

He nodded. "They were, and believe me it wasn't easy. She was all right. She understood I was helping, but not him; he's hard to get close to, that Micky."

I was too ashamed to say anything.

When I'd finished my tea, he said, "Well, are you up to telling me about how I murdered Flannagan, or will that have to wait for another day?"

I was still pretty woozy—and I mightn't have made much sense—but I told him all I could, starting from the visits of Mister right up to finding the boy in the cave.

"You sure that boy was sleeping?" was his only comment.

"He looked like he was."

"He might have been dead."

"There was a fire. I saw it. And we smelled food cooking. He can't have been dead if he just ate."

Pa shook his head. "No," he said, "I suppose not."

"But he must have been hungry sometimes. They say that he's been seen in town, raiding bins."

"I believe it. Just lately, he's been coming around here very late, one or two o'clock in the morning. Once I'd leave something out for him and he'd eat it all, but not lately. Whatever I leave out is still there when I get up, so I reckoned he must have been going somewhere else."

"I heard that he might have been jumping the milk trucks and getting a ride into town."

"He could, but he didn't have to, not if he wanted

food. If he was short of food he could have got it here. Besides, even if he was raiding bins, I don't think that's why he was in town. He went to town looking for her—for Leena—that's what I reckon."

"A few people say that. They say he might even have highly developed senses. . . ."

Pa got up when I started talking like that. "If you ever get to meet him, you'll find out what he can do, and what he can't. But right now, I think you should have a rest until your father comes, hey?"

"I've got one question," I said. "When Bobby left here, do you know where he was going?"

"No. He helped me carry you into the kitchen and then he made two phone calls. One was to get your father and the other was to the police, about the boy, I reckon, but it didn't make any sense to me at the time. After that, he went out to the car, brought in your backpack, and left."

I looked down at the watch pinned to my shirt. It was nearly ten o'clock. "What time was that?" I said.

"About nine. No more than five minutes after you arrived. He was in a big hurry. He never even cleaned your mess out of the car."

I was lying there when my father's car pulled up. Pa brought him in and he looked at my neck. I gathered that I wasn't going to die by the noises he made. He said, "You'll be okay."

When we went out to the car, Pa produced my backpack. I was happy about that because the fossils were in it, still in one piece, I hoped.

My father sat me in the front and I told him about finding the boy as soon as we were away—I thought it might save trouble later. But I needn't have bothered. Bobby had told my mother when he phoned and the sergeant had already warned them that he might be brought in.

"If they do catch him," I asked, "will you put him in that room with Leena?"

"That depends," he answered, which explained nothing.

I told him about the fossils and how I'd show them to everyone when I got home.

"We'll see," he said. "But you're not out of the woods yet. Not if you had five ticks pulled out of you."

I was put to bed as soon as I got home. By midday every muscle in my body ached and I had a high fever. My mother fussed over me, telling me that this was to be expected; that sometimes toxins took a few hours to pass through the system.

She took her upside-down watch off me, too, but when she put it back on her uniform, she said, "Well, look at that—it's stopped! And I've had it since you were a baby."

I didn't feel like a baby anymore.

Julia came and sat with me for a while. She didn't say a word about Bobby, so I got the impression that he was still unforgiven for not letting her go, but she told me a bit about Leena. That morning, the table had been pushed right over under her window.

"She's waiting," I said. "She knows that Micky's coming."

Julia laughed. "Don't be stupid. I made all that up just to scare you."

I could tell she was lying.

nineteen

Next morning I woke up to find the yard full of cars and trucks, including the Chevy, the police Landrover, and the yellow emergency vehicle used by the engineers at the dam. I guessed that they had captured the boy.

I went down to the kitchen. The sergeant was there, and two men from the emergency service, and Bobby of course, but nobody had any time for me. They were all having breakfast, unwillingly provided by Julia. When I hung around, trying to hear what was going on, they dropped their voices so low that I couldn't catch a word, or stopped talking altogether. Bobby knew that I was there, but pretended not to.

"Have they got him?" I asked Julia as she passed me with a tray.

She nodded. "He's in there with Leena. It looks like we're starting all over again."

"What's wrong with Bobby?" I said.

"How would I know? I'm not talking to him."

"I can see that. But why won't he talk to me?"

"Because he's too busy with the men to be bothered with a kid like you." She looked at him over her shoulder and added, "Can't you see? He found the wild boy. He's big time now. He's a hero."

I wandered out into the yard to look at the emergency truck. It was parked right next to the Chevy—which reminded me of how I'd been sick. I opened its back door, and the smell of stale vomit nearly knocked me over. This was the reason Bobby was ignoring me, I was sure.

I went straight back into the house for a bucket and some disinfectant. I'd make it up to him, I promised myself that.

When I came back, all loaded up and slopping water everywhere, there was Ben Cullen leaning on the front of the police car, having a smoke.

"Hello, Ben," I said. "How come you're out here?"

He flicked his ash onto the gravel. "Not wanted, am I?" he muttered.

"Not wanted? You were in on the capture, weren't you?"

I had no idea whether he was or he wasn't—I was trying to find out.

"Me?" he said with a sneer. "All I ever get is surveillance. Like this. The serge took me off this case when that bitch near ripped my eyes out in the Fergusons' henhouse."

"She's not really a bitch," I said. "Not when you get to know her."

I saw a change in his expression. "How do you mean, 'Get to know her'?"

I'd opened my big mouth again. He didn't know she was there. Like the others, he thought she'd been taken away. "She was here for a while," I said, but I was a hopeless liar.

He dropped his cigarette butt and crushed it beneath his boot. "No," he said, standing up to tower over me, "I don't reckon that's what you meant at all, is it?"

He reached out and pinched my ear, just enough to hurt.

I pulled away, spilling water down my leg. "She's been

staying here," I admitted. Now that Micky was caught, I thought he might as well know.

"What? All that time?"

I nodded.

"Well, well . . . so she didn't go down the coast?"

I shook my head. "She'll be with her brother now," I said. "And my parents, of course."

"Where?"

"There, see?" I pointed at the window. "But they won't be staying. My mother says it's not good for them, and it's too much for us. Welfare will be taking them soon, that's my guess."

This was all made up, but it sounded as if I knew what was going on.

"Yes," he said. "Welfare. That would be the best." He put his hands in his pockets and walked off, so I took it that our conversation was over.

I went over to the Chevy but he stopped, and said, "By the way, did they get all their stuff?"

"What stuff?"

"I noticed there were one or two personal items came in with that boy. Some clothes and stuff. And a suitcase. Young Bobby had it in his car. Did all that get taken in?"

"There was a suitcase up in the cave," I said, just to let him know that I'd been there too. He didn't take the hint so I added, "It could be in the Chevy. I'm just about to clean it. I can have a look."

"If it's no trouble," he said.

I opened the door but he pulled away fast when he caught a whiff. "Pong! Someone's chucked in here."

"That's why I'm cleaning it out," I said, not confessing responsibility.

He took the keys from the ignition and opened the trunk. There was nothing. "You reckon someone's taken it in?" he asked.

When I shrugged he put his hands back in his pockets and walked off again.

It took me the best part of an hour to clean up the car. Bobby came out with the other men just as I finished. When he saw what I had done he said, "Thanks, Kimbo," and got in without another word.

I thought that was pretty rude. I went to his door as he started up. "So, aren't you talking to me?" I asked.

He gave me a halfhearted grin. "Course I am. I already asked your mom if you were okay. But right now, me and the boys here have got business downtown."

Even I knew what that meant. They were going for a beer.

Later that afternoon the Fergusons arrived, along with Keithy. His parents went straight into the house but Keithy and I stayed out in the yard.

"I've got something to show you," he said. "Here, take a look."

The silver bike was lying in the back of their truck.

"I got that for Christmas," he grinned. "Isn't that something?"

"It's great," I said. "I wish I had one like it."

He looked at me in disbelief. "You could have one easy. My dad told me that your dad and mom make heaps. They could easy afford one. You've got all that other stuff up there." He nodded toward my room. "You should ask your dad."

I didn't respond to this and he took the hint. I think

most people thought that my father was a bit strange.

"Anyway," he said, "I'll get it out."

He jumped up onto the truck and passed the bike down to me. "You can take it for a ride around here if you want," he said, sweeping his arms wide to indicate the area enclosed by the wall. "You can't come to any harm in here."

I wasn't ready for this and put up a defense. "No thanks," I said. "I was sick last night. I don't think I'm up to it."

"Up to it? I'm not saying you should ride it to the coast and back. Just around here, see?"

"I might pee on the seat," I joked.

He didn't laugh. He came up very close and looked me in the eye. "Hey," he said, "I reckon that you can't ride . . . that's the trouble, isn't it?"

He read the answer in my face.

He took a couple of turns around the yard himself, then we put the bike away and sat on the kitchen step for a drink.

"It's a funny business about that boy," he said.

I knew straight off that he had a story to tell, but he always needed prompting. "What?" I asked. "Him getting caught?"

"I mean, *how* he got caught."

"Have you heard?" I said.

"Course I heard. Haven't you?"

I had to sound convincing without admitting that I knew nothing. "A bit," I hedged, "about the emergency team . . ."

This was not altogether a lie. The men had eaten in our kitchen and the truck had been parked in our yard. "Why, what did you hear?"

"Well . . ." he stretched his legs and gave a little sigh, then began. "They reckon the first information they had that he was found came when Bobby O'Meara phoned the police. They phoned your dad to say they might need his help. Now I can't be sure of all this, and I know you might have heard different, but I'm just telling you what I was told, all right?"

I said that was all right.

"They reckon Bobby phoned from Pa Cossey's place. Next thing, he drove up to the dam and convinced the emergency team, face to face, that they might be needed. He said that a boy was trapped on a ledge at the fourth Thumb, and one false move and he'd be dead. They didn't fool around after that, they took off with Bobby leading the way. The cops met them at the turnoff to the old loggers' road."

Keithy stopped at this point. "Now, I don't know that area myself," he admitted, "but they say there was trouble getting access to that particular side of the Thumbs. One way was to go down the loggers' road—which meant crossing the dam—and the other was to go over the ridge that separates the North Arm swamp from the Thumbs, through the valley, that is, and then around. Can you understand that?"

I nodded. I understood better than he knew. So far my part in this drama hadn't got a mention.

"After they talked about it they took Bobby's advice and went in from the other side, across the water. They had rubber inflatables on the emergency vehicle, see. But they reckon that Bobby had gone across himself, using a homemade raft—made of fuel tins and a gate. A gate! How about that?"

I thought of what Julia had said about Bobby being a big man and a hero; now I began to understand.

"Anyway," Keithy went on, "they made it across all right, but the real trouble started when they got to the rescue site—which was a cave halfway into the mountain. Now, they reckon there was one detail that Bobby had overlooked—on purpose maybe . . ."

I sat up, thinking that this could be me.

"When Bobby found that boy, he was asleep on a ledge, and to stop him getting away Bobby pulled up the tree root that he used to go in and out. That was nearly two hours before, see, but now the boy wasn't asleep anymore—he was screaming and roaring, and pacing up and down that ledge like a wild animal. That's when the emergency team worked out this wasn't any ordinary boy—up till then, they thought it was just some kid that Bobby had gone up there with, camping out, see, for the weekend."

According to Bobby, I didn't exist, that's what I saw.

"So then they got the full picture: This crazy kid screaming his head off, he was the wild boy that they'd heard so much about. The Flannagan kid. But the trouble was, they couldn't just walk away and leave him there. He couldn't just stay there by himself. Everyone agreed on that, except for that bastard Ben Cullen, who said he couldn't see why not, and he got sent back to keep an eye on the inflatables for saying so.

"They had lots of different ideas, but none were any good—like tear gas, which they would have to send to the coast for and even then he might just throw himself over; or lowering a platform and chucking a net on him, but they didn't have a net, except the one back on the emergency truck way over on the loggers' inlet. So just when it looked like they would have to call up the army, one of the emergency team boys suggested a stun gun—the sort that fires sedatives into animals. He reckoned there was a deer farmer up Colliston way who had one.

"It took three hours for the gun to be brought in and the deer farmer came with it. He wanted witnesses to clear his name if things went wrong.

"The boy had been quiet for a while, just lying there watching them—like an animal does, see, when it's all in—but when he saw that gun turn up, and saw it get loaded, he had the brains to work out it was curtains for him and he started screaming again. I heard that he would have gone over, chucked himself straight over the edge, only for the serge hitting him fast. He staggered around for ten or fifteen seconds, I got told—my dad heard it was longer—and then he went down like a sack of potatoes. One shot in the neck, right behind the ear, right into a vein it went, and he was out of it. Finished. Good as dead."

I thanked Keithy for telling me the story. I didn't say that I'd been up there myself, and could have described the caves better. He would have thought I was showing off, trying to make up for the fact that I couldn't ride a bike.

twenty

the boy recovered from the effects of the stun gun without any trouble. After one day he was "sitting up and taking notice," my mother said, but I wasn't allowed to see him until the second day, when I was told that it was all right to go in.

Leena was on the floor behind the door, wrapped up in a blanket. I expected the silent treatment, but I was wrong. Instead, she put her finger to her lips to tell me to be quiet. I soon saw why. Black hair was sticking out from the blanket near her shoulder, and I guessed that it was him, hiding.

"Will I come back?" I whispered.

She shook her head. "He's scared," she said. "But you can stay."

I sat down on the floor near the table and leaned against its leg, just as I had that first time I saw her. I could see some of his face and thought that he was watching me.

She talked to him all the while, the same way some children talk to dolls. "This is Kimmy," she said. "He's a friend. He's a boy, like you. Just like you. He lives in this big house. You saw him here another time. Did you know that? One time we came with the parrots, remember? When the Fadder cut his arm real bad."

All this time she rocked him, as mothers with babies

do, until she lifted her hand and slowly opened the blue silk edge of the blanket.

His face was as sharp as a pixie's, with arched eyebrows, blackcurrant eyes, and a wide red mouth. Spikes of straight black hair stood up all over his head.

I held out my hand, but Leena's eyes said "no" and I sat back.

Leena took care of Micky. She washed him; she taught him to use the toilet; she supervised his eating, even coming into the kitchen to help prepare his food; but by the end of the third day we could see that he would have to go, and the sooner the better.

First, he refused to wear clothes. No matter what Leena was given to dress him in—which included a pajama shirt of my father's—he tore it off. The only thing that he would keep on was a pair of my shorts that fitted just right around his waist. He had been wearing the remains of a similar pair when he was brought in, but my mother had soon disposed of them.

The second problem was that he hated being in the room. Micky needed space. Like Pa said, he wasn't at all like Leena.

He had no idea what a book was—he just ripped them up. Once I tried to interest him in drawing, but he jabbed the pencil into my wrist so far that my mother had to treat me.

He entertained himself by jumping on the beds and later, when he learned how, by jumping from bed to bed, a distance of over four yards.

On the third day, between bouts of manic energy, he pushed the table over to the window and sat there, gripping the bars and staring out.

He never spoke. He could make animal noises, and certainly he could laugh, but nothing else. Nobody except me seemed to notice this: Pa hadn't mentioned it, nor did the men who captured him, nor did my parents. I supposed that everybody thought he was too frightened. So I watched him and Leena together and started to wonder.

"He doesn't talk much," I said to her. "Do you think he's still a bit scared?"

"Could be that," she said.

On the fourth day, when she was in the kitchen, I made up my mind to find out. Apples were Micky's favorite food. I purposely chose a bright red one and held it out to him.

I said, "Say please, Micky. Say please and you can have it."

He usually obeyed, but not this time. All he had to do was say the word and I would have given it to him. He couldn't. I saw him try. I saw him shape his mouth and form his tongue, all ready, but nothing came out, only an ugly grunt.

"Can you say please, Micky?" I encouraged him. "Can you?"

When I heard Leena at the door, I gave the apple to him.

"That's not right," she said, seeing him eating it. "I got his dinner here. Now he's got that."

"I'm sure he'll eat both," I said. I think he would have eaten the magazines if he could.

She began to spoon his dinner into his mouth.

"Leena," I said, "can he talk, really?"

"Course he can," she snapped.

"But he's been here four days," I said, "and I haven't heard a word. Or not one I can understand."

She kept on shoveling food down his throat.

"It's a bit hard to be his friend if I can't talk to him," I said.

"You wait and see," Leena whispered. "He'll talk when he wants to."

twenty-one

My parents' problems weren't confined to Leena and Micky. They still had Julia to contend with and, with the New Year, the prospect of sending her away to boarding school.

One morning at breakfast my mother said, "Julia, the 'Mother and Daughter Orientation Day' for new boarders is on the twelfth. With all the fuss going on here, I'd forgotten. We have to go down. It's an obligation."

Julia made her usual face at the mention of school. "Do we really have to?"

"Yes," my father said.

My mother saw a situation brewing. "It's nothing," she said. "We could be down and back in the day."

"But how long do we have to stay at the school?"

"As long as it takes. I imagine there's some sort of address to all the new girls, and then a tour of the school. You have to see the boarding facilities, Julia. And find your place in the dorm."

The idea that Julia would be sleeping with other girls had never occurred to me. I always imagined that she'd have a room of her own, looking out over an English garden, like the head prefects in my books.

"Would we go on the bus?" I could tell she was working up to something.

"What else? Your father needs the car."

"Well then," she pushed away her uneaten toast, "since

it looks as if I really am going . . ." She paused, on the off-chance that someone would deny it. ". . . I want you to do something for me. When we—"

My father put down his coffee, cutting her off. "Something for you? We're already doing something for you. What do you think all this boarding school business is about?"

"If you took the time to think about it," she replied, quite calmly, "you would recall that I, personally, don't want to go."

I sometimes wondered, when Julia was at her dramatic best, if she rehearsed in front of a mirror.

"Go on," my mother said, "do *what* for you?"

Julia folded her hands on the table and proceeded. "Seeing you're determined to get rid of me, I was wondering, since we're already going to be down there, if we could do it properly? I mean, instead of getting the bus home that afternoon, which is awful and makes everything a big rush, why don't we take our time, and have dinner, and go to a movie and stay the night in a hotel?" She allowed this to register, then added, "A really good hotel."

My father recovered first. "Ridiculous," he muttered.

My mother looked at him in surprise. "Why is it ridiculous, Ivan? There's nothing ridiculous in a mother spending time with her daughter. Especially when she's about to lose her. I think it's a wonderful idea."

"What about the other pair?" he said. "If there's an emergency, who's going to look after them?"

"Leena seems to be doing quite well," my mother said.

"And there's me," I offered.

He pushed back his chair. "Helen," he said, "if you

want to go out for an evening, I'm sure that I can't stop you."

Nobody spoke until he had left the room; then my mother turned to Julia. "All right. If that's what you want, I'll be in it. But you have to do something for me."

Julia's face fell. "What?" she said flatly.

"I'm leaving the organization to you. The bus tickets. The restaurant bookings. The hotel. You say you want to be a manager. Well, all right, here's your chance. I certainly haven't got the time."

Julia was delighted. When my mother had gone, she said, "Kimmy, I never thought I'd get away with that one. And I made it all up on the spot."

Then she disappeared too, leaving me with the breakfast dishes.

Micky's dinner was always made early and one afternoon, well before dark, he was left alone while Leena helped prepare it. She hadn't bothered to lock the door—she was only at the other end of the hall—but when she came back with his tray the room was empty.

In no time we were all in the reception room, working out who would look where. My mother took upstairs, my father downstairs and the cellar. Julia did the front yard. I took the back and outside the wall, since I could run fastest.

Leena was hopeless. She sat in the room and cried.

The house was filled with the sound of Micky's name, but he didn't answer and couldn't be found.

My father called the police. It was just our luck that Ben Cullen was on duty.

He swaggered into the reception room and sat on my

mother's desk. "So," he began, "you let him get away, hey?"

Nobody responded.

"You're liable, you know," he continued, staring around the room as if he was half-expecting to discover Micky there. "You realize that it was your responsibility to keep him locked up."

My father couldn't resist. "Is that so? We were under the impression that he was here on holiday."

Stupid as he was, Ben got the message. "Well," he said, smoothing back his greasy hair, "I'd better take a look around."

"We've already done that," my mother explained. "Otherwise we wouldn't have called."

He drew himself up, ignoring her. "Doc, civilians have their way of doing things. The force has another."

"I'm sure it has," my father said. "That's why I'm ringing the sergeant at home."

When he heard that, Ben took out his notebook and went into the yard.

I couldn't stand doing nothing. "I'm going up into the eyrie," I said. "I might spot him from there."

"Oh sure," Julia sneered. "Except he'd be halfway to the Thumbs by now."

"For all you know," I said, "I might be able to see that far."

As it turned out I didn't have to look at all. As soon as I lifted the trapdoor into the eyrie, I saw Micky crouched by the railings, staring out toward the hills.

"Micky," I said, "we've been looking for you everywhere."

He grinned in his silly sort of way.

"Now you come down," I ordered, grabbing his arm

and dragging him back. "You're very bad, running away like that. You wait till Leena gets hold of you."

Like everybody else, I had slipped into the habit of talking to him like a dog.

Later, when the sergeant arrived, my parents sat in the kitchen and had a long talk.

"We can't go on like this," my mother said. "Leena's all right, but not Micky. He has to go."

My father shook his head. "No, they both have to go. Not because we want to get rid of them, but because we can't do any more for them. They're both healthy, we've seen to that, but now Micky's here, she's not progressing. For a while I thought that Kim was getting somewhere, but not now. All her energy is devoted to Micky. All she wants to do is baby him. And she hasn't got that sort of maturity. This morning was a good case. In a genuine emergency, she went to pieces and sat in there crying."

"And there's his speech," my mother added. "Leena says he can talk, but we've never heard him. He needs specialist help with that; he needs a therapist . . . but I don't want them separated. And I don't want them stuck in institutions either. If Leena lost him again it would kill her, I'm sure of it."

My father ran his hands through his hair. "That's the problem, Helen. While Micky stays with her, he won't develop. I think that might be the trouble with his speech. Maybe he can talk, but because she does everything for him, he doesn't need to. He just has to look at her and she acts. As if he's a baby, don't you see?"

The sergeant understood. "I'll get on to welfare again," he said. "I didn't expect any word until the New Year, but we should be able to get some action now."

When my parents walked the sergeant to his car, I saw that Julia and Ben had been talking, too.

"What was that all about?" I said when she came back into the house.

She laughed. "You wouldn't believe it, but Constable Cullen made a pass at me. He came over and said, 'Now that you're not going with Bobby O'Meara, how would you like to go out with me?'"

"What's he mean that you're not going with Bobby?"

She shrugged. "It looks like everybody knows that we had a fight."

"Who said so?"

"Bobby, I guess."

I couldn't believe my ears. "What? It's over with Bobby because you wanted to go up to the Thumbs with him?"

"No. It was more than that. Bobby has been wanting to hang around with the boys for a while. I knew that way back at the Spring Dance . . . you remember . . . and since I'm going down to school anyway, it might as well end now . . . but I've given him something to think about."

"What's that supposed to mean?"

"I told Ben to call me after the twelfth. I said we'd be down the coast till then."

"You're lying. You wouldn't ever go out with Ben Cullen . . . would you?"

She laughed again. "Of course not. I told him to call me, that's all. I'd sooner be dead than be seen with him. But he'll tell Bobby we're going out—or something worse, something filthy probably—just to stir Bobby up. And that suits me."

twenty-two

When my mother and Julia finally left for their "Mother and Daughter Day" I spent my time with Leena and Micky. My father was busy in the office and with all the cars coming and going in the yard, Micky was happy to sit on the table and look out. Leena was learning to play dominoes, a game she was very good at, since she was fast at figures and even faster at recognizing any sort of pattern.

"You're terrific," I said when she beat me for the third time. "You wait, when you get to school, I bet you turn out to be a mathematical genius."

"I'll never get to school," she said.

"Of course you will. Why shouldn't you?"

"Because of him." She nodded toward Micky, rocking by the window.

"You wait," I said. "I bet you do."

She looked at me carefully. "Are they coming to get us soon?" she whispered.

I hadn't meant to threaten her. I tried to cover my mistake. "I meant one day you'll get back to school again. I didn't mean now. . . ."

"When are they coming?" she said.

"I don't know," I admitted. "I heard them talking after Micky ran away. That's all. They're waiting to hear from the welfare people."

"They'll take him away from me, won't they?"

"I don't know," I said again. "I can't answer all that. But they'll be kind, and they'll know how to help him. That's their job."

"Some people already tried." I could tell she didn't believe me, even before she spoke.

"You mean like Pa?"

"Pa? Who's Pa?"

"Pa Cossey. From up the dam. He pulled out your ticks. You got the candlenuts off him."

She smiled. "You mean Cossey. I called him Cossey. I remember him, he was all right. But he couldn't settle Micky. And he tried."

"Who else tried?"

"Different people. Different ladies the Fadder lived with. Like Moira."

"Was Moira Micky's mother?"

She squirmed when I asked that. Finally she said, "I don't know where Micky came from. One night I went to sleep and the next morning he was there, see. . . ."

"He's not your baby is he?" I whispered.

She covered her mouth and laughed. "No. I never had a baby. I never had a man in me, not like you do to make babies. But I looked after him, from when I was a little girl. He's like my baby."

"But he has to learn. He has to . . ."

"You don't listen," she said, shaking her head. "I'm telling you, he's different. He's from out there. Up in the hills and in the caves. There's nothing you can teach him if he doesn't want to learn. I knew that a long time ago."

I looked down at the dominoes, standing end to end.

She had built a wall between us. Not much of one, but a wall all the same.

After dinner, my father went down to the cellar and I took strawberry ice cream into Leena's room for dessert.

It was very hot. From the west, way out past the Angel's Gate, a summer storm was brewing. At odd times there were flashes of lightning, and Micky leaped up onto his table to watch.

"I could take you both up to the roof," I suggested, "but it might get dangerous. We're safer down here."

"We been in plenty of storms," Leena said, "just under a sheet of tin. We're not worried about this."

The rain started about eight o'clock. It was so heavy that I went around the house shutting the windows, just in case.

I'd hardly finished, when the phone rang in the reception room. I ran down, thinking that it might be my mother, or Julia ringing from their hotel at the coast. It was Mr. Riley, a farmer from out Wyvenhoe way: His wife had been feeding the pigs when a bolt of lightning hit the sty. "She's not hit," he said, "but she got a terrible fright, and now her heart's going like crazy. Can the Doc come, quick?"

I knocked on the cellar door. When my father came up, I told him what had happened as fast as I could.

"I'll have to go," he said. "Will you be all right?"

If I'd said "no," Mrs. Riley might die.

"I'll look after them," I assured him as he left.

The rain pelted down and the wind howled all about the house. The Laurels always took the full brunt of storms, especially if they blew in through the Angel's

Gate, but I couldn't recall anything as wild as this. I was afraid for my father, driving through it, all the way out to the Rileys'.

I said to Leena, "This is very bad. I'd better double-check the windows. If one blows open, there could be a terrible mess."

I ran upstairs and went into every room, checking that each window was securely latched and pulling the curtains closed. My mother always did this in case a window shattered, and the slivers of glass were blown back into the house.

I heard the sound of metal against metal and saw sheets of tin from the garage roof tear off and spin end over end into the storm. I saw my branch in the laurel break away.

I daren't look anymore. I drew the curtains and ran down the stairs, but when I reached the hall the lights began to flicker, and by the time I got to Leena's room, they had failed completely, leaving the house in darkness.

After that, the three of us sat on the table, looking out into the night.

In an hour the worst was over. The wind fell and the rain was no more than a drizzle.

"There's some candles in the kitchen," I said. "I'll bring them in."

I was making my way to the door when Leena called after me, "What about getting another game? I'm sick of dominoes."

"Sure," I said. "That'll cheer us up." There were plenty of board games in the living room sideboard.

I groped down the hall, through the reception room, and into the kitchen. I found the candles and a holder in the cupboard under the sink, and the matches in the cutlery drawer. As I lit a candle, I congratulated myself on how well I had handled the crisis. My parents would have been proud.

Holding the candle high, I went into the living room, collected an armful of games, and made my way back to the children's room. In the doorway, I held the candle beneath my jaw to cast a ghastly light up under my face, and wailed, "I'm heeerrr . . . I'm heeerrr . . ." in my scariest voice.

I expected a reaction from inside; a giggle, or a squeal, but there was nothing.

Embarrassed, I tried again. "I'm heeerrr . . ."

Again, nothing. I held the candle high and stepped into the room. Leena was in her corner and Micky with her, huddled against her shoulder.

"What's wrong?" I said.

From the shadows came the faintest whisper: "Mister . . ."

"Where?" I demanded. "Where is he?"

As I spoke, I heard the sound of boots on gravel.

I was determined not to be afraid. I put the board games down and climbed onto the table. I cupped my hand around the candle flame, and peered out through the bars.

At first I could only make out my own face staring back at me, and I held the candle away from the glass. When I looked again, I had a dim view of the yard. To my right I could make out nothing, but when I turned toward the kitchen, I saw something move.

I put the candle down. By pressing my head hard against the bars, I managed to see the full length of the back of the house. There, moving among the shadows, I saw the figure of a man.

All the windows were latched and barred. All the doors were locked. But he was looking lower than any windows or doors. He was looking just above the ground. And then, at a spot a yard or so past the kitchen door, he dropped to his knees. I wondered, what would he want down there? A key? Was he looking for the place where we hid a key? In a potted plant maybe, or beneath a mat?

But when he began to push, I knew. When he dropped flat onto his stomach, and began to disappear, I knew. It was the window to the cellar he'd been after. It was the only window that remained unbarred.

I had no idea who this man was, but I was certain of one thing. It wasn't me he was after. It was them, huddled in the corner. And it was them that I had to protect.

There was no lock on the cellar door, not even a latch. The best that I could do was keep him out of this room. It had a lock, and a good one too, an old one. All I had to do was go out into the hall, and lock them in. It was simple.

But to do that, I had to lock myself out. With him.

I said nothing to Leena. I snuffed the candle and slipped off the table, then closed the door and locked it behind me. I put the key in my pocket.

The hall was pitch dark. I could go into the single room next door, and hide in there, or get beneath the desk in the reception room. I could even use the phone. I took two steps in that direction, but as I did, I heard the cellar door swing open. The hall closet was behind me. I opened the door and stepped in.

I heard the creak of leather boots coming closer.

I heard the rattle of a doorknob.

"Open this door," a voice said, very soft. "Open this door before I get mad."

I knew then who Mister was. I should have known all the time. I opened the door and stepped out behind him.

"Ben Cullen," I said, "you leave them alone."

I never saw anyone move like he did. He spun around and dropped to one knee. I caught the glint of metal. He had a revolver aimed at me.

"You," he said, peering into the dark. "What are you doing here?"

I stood my ground, but I didn't answer him.

He got up and came closer, prodding my chest with the gun. "How come you're not away? Your sister said you were away. . . ."

I'd known Ben Cullen for as long as I could remember; since my mother first put my playpen in the reception room and I'd seen him blubbering on the settee, waiting for my father to set his broken arm; since I was in the first grade, and he bashed little kids to get their lunch money; since Julia had told me what he did to Maureen Peed. I wasn't scared of Ben Cullen, even if he was Mister.

"It doesn't look like I went away, does it?" I said. "And you better put that stupid gun away. If you fired it, they'd trace the bullet in a minute. Any cop would know that."

He stepped back, and lifted the gun above my head, as if he would strike me. "You little faggot," he said. "You miserable little . . ."

A series of threats followed, none of which I distinctly heard. Beneath his voice I had caught another sound:

The sound of tires on gravel; the drone of an engine. A car had turned into our yard. The sergeant's four-wheel drive, I was certain.

I knew exactly what to do.

"Don't you call me a faggot," I said, walking backward. "I'm not the one who needs a uniform to make him a man. I'm not the one who gets put off the job. I'm not the one who holds up a kid with a gun . . . don't you call me a faggot. . . ."

I was in the reception room. I heard a key turn in the door. I continued to lead him on.

". . . I know who's a fag. . . . So does everyone in this town. . . ."

Then the door swung open and my father was there. "Kim . . ." he said, spotting me in the half light, ". . . are you all right? The car broke down and the sergeant gave me a lift. . . . What? Have we lost the lights?" As he spoke Sergeant Mortimer entered the reception room behind him.

Ben lowered the gun to his side, but he was too late. We were out of the dark tunnel of the hall. My father saw him, and the sergeant too. "What the . . ." he stammered.

Ben tried to reach the door, but my father stepped forward, blocking him. "What's going on here?" he demanded. He looked from me to Ben. "What are you doing with that gun? Tell me . . ." But as he spoke the sergeant pushed past, and as he did, Ben lost his nerve. The gun fell from his hand, hitting the carpet with a thud. He dropped down on the settee and buried his face in his hands. The room was filled with the sound of his sobbing.

234 gary crew

The sergeant showed no sympathy. "Sit up," he said, "sit up and behave like a man. Answer the question. What are you doing here? Tell me!" As he spoke he bent down and picked up the gun.

Ben looked up, his face contorted. "Please Serge," he sniveled, "I've done nothing. Honest . . ."

I couldn't stand this. "That's a lie," I said. "When the lights went, he came in here through the cellar window. He came right through the house, with that gun, after them. . . ."

I saw my father stiffen. He'd forgotten the others.

". . . But I locked their door, so he couldn't get them; so he got me, in the hall. . . ."

"Is that true?" the sergeant said. "Is it?" He turned the gun in his hand—whether by design or accident, I will never know—but the muzzle pointed toward Ben.

"Don't. Please . . ." he wailed, motioning the gun away. "I'll tell. I'll tell you everything. I swear."

At this, my father stepped forward. He knelt in front of me and put his hands on my shoulders. "Are those children all right?" he asked.

"Yes," I answered.

He stood and turned to Ben. "Was this about them?"

Ben nodded.

"Then we'll have it out, here and now. Kim, you bring the children out. I'm going down to start the generator, then at least we'll have some light. Sergeant, you'll keep an eye on our visitor, here, won't you?"

There was no protest.

I found Leena and Micky huddled in the dark, exactly as before. "It's only me," I said. "My father's come home. And the sergeant's with him. Everything's all right."

As I spoke the dull rumble of the generator starting filled the house. Seconds later, the lights flickered on.

"See?" I coaxed, "it's all over. You can come out now. Come on. My father wants you. Out here . . ." and little by little I led them from the room and down the hall; Micky needing no second invitation, Leena lagging behind, dragging the blanket.

My father was waiting when we reached the reception room. "There's someone here to meet you," he said in his no-nonsense way.

When the children saw Ben, they stepped back at once; Leena hissing "Mister," through her teeth.

"What did she say?" the sergeant asked.

"Mister," I said.

My father understood. "So. This is the mysterious Mister, is it? Well, well. Mister is the one who's been terrifying the children," he said to the sergeant. "They have nightmares about him."

The sergeant planted his feet wide and folded his arms across his chest. "Great example for a cop to set. So, are you going to explain here or at the station?"

"It was a joke," Ben said. "That's how it—"

"A joke?" my father cut in. "Do you know the terror 'Mister' has caused in the lives of these two?"

"It was their own father started it, not me. 'Mister Big' he called me. Then all this other stuff started, scaring them with all these stories, but it wasn't me doing it, it was their own father. Ask her, she knows."

"Is that true, Leena?" My father was very firm. "We have to sort all this out."

"The Fadder always called him Mister. He'd say, 'You watch out. That Mister's comin' over tonight. And he's after you.' When he said that, we'd clear out and hide, me and Micky. We always knew it was Mister by his boots. These big black boots. We'd hear him coming down through the bush. And if we played up, the Fadder said Mister would come and take us away. That's what the Fadder said about Mister; that's what he said, exactly."

"It was a game," Ben protested. "He only did it to scare the crap out of them."

The sergeant smiled a thin smile. "So . . . if you're so all-fired innocent, what were you doing here tonight, terrifying the daylights out of them?"

"I came to get something. Something that's mine." He looked across and caught Leena staring. "Don't you stare at me like I'm some kinda freak," he started in. "I know who's the freak—"

The sergeant silenced him. "Shut up," he said. "You're in no position to abuse anybody. Leena, do you know what he's talking about?"

She shook her head. "Lots of men came to see the Fadder. We never hung around, Micky and me. I didn't want them looking at me."

"There. She doesn't know what you're here for. And the boy . . ." he turned to my father, "He doesn't talk, does he? No. So it looks like it's up to you, Constable. We're waiting."

Ben lifted his head. "All right," he said. "All right. But don't think that I'm taking all the blame. It was Flannagan too. I got conned by him, just like half the other suckers in this town, see?" He stared at us all, still defiant.

"I'm waiting," was all the sergeant said. The gun glimmered in his hands.

Ben curled his lip. "I heard," he muttered. "I met Flannagan in the pub one night, and he told me about this vein called the Bullion Run. He said he had a map of where it was—somewhere in the hills above the dam—but it was deep, he said, with a lot of overburden, and he was too old to work it. I didn't believe him, but when I started drinking with him, back at his camp up the North Arm, he showed me this gold. Not nuggets—like he showed Van Marseveen and them at the inquest—this was still in the rock, like it really did come from a seam. I went back a few times, just to talk to him, and have another look, and every time, he did this Mister thing with the kids. Like she said, he'd make out like I was coming to take them away, and he'd stir them up and scare the hell out of them.

"Anyway, after a few nights of this, I went up with the money . . . and you might as well know . . . that was the night he got murdered. I'm saying that straight out, just so you know . . . I'd been drinking a bit before I went up, tossing this whole map idea around—saying, 'Will I? Won't I?'—but when I got up there, I saw this other vehicle. I thought, *hello, what's he up to here?* It was late, and I went down very quietly to have a look.

"When I'm nearly there, I walked right into this pair, these kids here. They were hiding in the bushes. I grabbed hold of them and told them to be quiet, and they did, no trouble. I think they were scared to death that Mister really had come to get them. But when these other guys left, I let them go.

"I went up to Flannagan and handed over the money. Five hundred bucks I gave him. Cash. He took off with it into that lean-to they all lived under, opened up this dirty old suitcase he had there and put the money inside the lining, beneath the lid. When he came back I asked him for the map.

"He said, 'You come and see me the same time tomorrow, and I'll have your map.' I said that I wanted it then, but he wouldn't hand it over. He said it was too valuable to keep around the camp; he had it stashed in a safe place.

"I guess I was a bit under the weather—but I knew then that this was a con; now he had my money he'd take off—so I started to rough him up. Nothing dangerous, honest, just enough to let him know who was boss—and that's when it got out of hand. . . ." He dropped his head, and buried his face in his hands.

The sergeant offered some help. ". . . And then you killed him?"

Ben looked up. "No, Serge," he said. "I never killed him."

I heard my father sigh. "Well then, who the blazes did?"

Micky had been sitting next to me, listening. When my father said this, he stood up and stepped forward.

"I did," he said. "I kill da Fadder."

From deep in the cellar I heard the faint hum of the generator. All else was silence.

Leena reached over and touched Micky's hand, drawing him to her.

"He didn't mean to," she whispered. "Micky loved the Fadder. He was the only one that Micky would speak to."

My father was watching her with dismay. "Did he do it? Did Micky do it?"

"Yes," she said, "but it was an accident. He meant to hit Mister."

"That's why you ran?"

"Not right then. When the Fadder fell down, we heard someone coming down the track and went back into the bushes. He did too." She pointed at Ben. "It was one of them workers from the dam. He never hardly looked at the Fadder, he just picked up some keys lying on the ground and went.

"But the Fadder was dead, I could tell, and Mister was right there. I thought, *We're gone. This Mister, he's going to take us now.* But he didn't do anything. He didn't touch us. He took off straight away. Soon as the one with the keys went, Mister went too. I said to Micky, 'He'll be back. He'll be back to get us,' then we grabbed what we could and stuffed it in that bag and we went. Right up to the Thumbs, we went, into the caves, and that's where we should have stayed . . . because we're done now. They'll take us away now," and she held Micky close.

My father moved to reassure her, but the sergeant turned to Ben. "I don't understand you," he said. "You knew all of this, and yet you let those men stand up there at that inquiry . . . you let those people suffer. Did you know that one of them has suicided? What sort of a man are you?"

Ben said nothing, but my father had been taking all of this in. "Kim," he said, "when Micky was brought here, I saw Bobby carry a suitcase in. Did you see what happened to it?"

I was about to say "no," when Leena answered, "It's under my bed. Julia put it there."

"Ben says he saw your father hide money in it. Did you find it?"

She shook her head. "I never knew about any money."

"Bring that case out," he said.

There was an awkward silence while she was gone, but she was back in no time, a battered suitcase in her hand. "There," she said, dropping it at Ben's feet. "Show us then."

He undid the catches and opened it. Inside it was lined with striped cotton, stained and rotten. His hand slipped down between this and the lid. I saw it close on something.

"It's still there," he said, pulling out a cream-colored envelope. "Now do you believe me? This is what I was after. Not them. I just wanted them to tell me where it was, that's all. It's got my name on it. That's why I wanted it." The envelope carried the symbol of the state police; beneath that was Ben's name, typed in capital letters. "It's my pay packet, see?"

He opened the envelope and removed a pile of bills; fifties and hundreds. It was a lot of money, I could see that. "It's all here," he said. "Five hundred dollars."

Then he did the strangest thing. He divided the money in half, and held out one hand to my father, the other to the sergeant. "Here," he said. "If you forget what you saw tonight, it's yours. Okay?"

My father backed away, repulsed, but the sergeant laughed. "You never give up, do you? Now you're adding attempted bribery of a police officer to your list of offenses. Withholding evidence. Entering. Misuse of police weapons. . . . I'd say I could even make a kidnapping charge stick, if I tried. No, better keep your money. You're going to need plenty for court costs, I reckon. Come on, let's go. . . ." He reached out and dragged Ben from the settee. "Sorry about all this, Doc," he said. "And you, too, kids. I reckon I should have done something about my constable awhile ago. . . ." He was heading for the door, with Ben in tow, but I couldn't let him leave, not like that.

"What about Micky?" I asked. "What will happen to him? Since he . . ." I wanted to say "Since he killed the Fadder," but I couldn't form the words.

The sergeant shook his head. "Leave it with me. I'll be in touch with Coroner Crisp. She'll handle it right. I know she will." He opened the door for Ben to go ahead, then he stopped, and called back to my father. "I'll phone you in the morning, Doc. After I've taken this one down to City Office." He closed the door behind him.

I never saw Ben Cullen after that.

When my father had settled the children, he came up to my room. "Kim," he called from the door.

"I'm in bed," I answered.

"You know, if you can't sleep, you can hop in with me."

"I'm not scared," I said. "I'm okay in here."

He came to stand beside me. "Kimmy," he whispered, "you were very brave tonight. You made me proud."

And bending down, he stroked my hair.

twenty-three

As soon as the bus from the coast pulled in the following afternoon my father took my mother to one side and spoke to her in private. I was even more surprised when he came into the kitchen, kissed Julia and myself, and drove off.

"What was that all about?" Julia asked. "He didn't even want to know what we did."

"It's about the children," my mother said. "I think Kimmy might have something to tell us."

They left their bags and sat at the kitchen table to hear the story. I told it as honestly as I could and answered all their questions without exaggeration.

"Anyway," I concluded, "if you don't believe me, you can check with Leena."

My father didn't come home that night and we were given no explanation of his absence. "Just wait and see," my mother said. Julia and I considered this with some suspicion.

"It's all very odd," she said. "Mom takes a night off, then he does too. Too much of a coincidence, don't you think? Does this mean divorce?"

She was being silly, I knew, but I hated being told to "wait and see."

He came home at lunchtime the next day. I heard him pull into the drive and went out. The car was covered with mud.

"How did that happen?" I asked.

He looked back as if he hadn't noticed. "I've been out through the Angel's Gate," he said. "It's wild country out there."

When he'd spoken to my mother he called everyone, including Leena and Micky, into the living room. He was standing by the fireplace, and looked very formal.

"First thing yesterday," he began, "Ms. Cuttler from welfare phoned to say that they were coming. She said that they'd be here today. . . . By that, she meant to have you ready." He glanced at Leena and Micky, who were sitting together on the floor.

"In the circumstances, I drove straight out to Wintery Hill, to your uncle's place. . . ."

Leena made a face. "I know all about him," she said. "He's a proper bastard. That's what our Fadder said."

My father nodded. "Yes. That's a reasonable assessment. But I wanted you to know that I tried. As your father's brother, he's your next of kin, the closest relative that you have. I just wanted to be sure that he wouldn't take you—or that he wasn't fit to take you—one of the two. It turned out to be both, I'm afraid. But I wanted you to know that I tried."

Nobody spoke for a minute, then Leena piped up.

"You did the right thing, Doc. And you always did. Even for our Fadder. I saw what you did when he cut his arm. You stitched that up real well. And I know that I called you for everything when I got brought in, but I was wrong. I know that now." She looked around at us all. "You all did the right thing. Even you, in the end." She said this to Julia, who blushed.

"Ms. Cuttler and Dr. Tiffin will be here this afternoon," my mother said. "But Leena . . . it is the right thing, as you say."

When they went back to the room to get ready, I phoned Pa. I had never told anyone about his part in all this.

"I'll be in," he said. "Don't let them go until I get there. Stall them if you have to."

He arrived as Ms. Cuttler and Dr. Tiffin pulled up in their station wagon. He made out that he had just come in to do the yard and disappeared into the garage to watch.

My parents signed a few papers, then Leena and Micky came out. Micky was wearing a pair of my shorts and a shirt of my father's that hung out all the way around. He had nothing on his feet. Leena wore a pair of my mother's tennis shoes and a dress of Julia's. It was cornflower blue.

We had offered her a new suitcase but she refused. "This one was good enough for the Fadder, so it'll do us," she said. In the space beneath the lining she had packed her precious Christmas paper.

Micky jumped into the back seat of the station wagon without hesitation, but Leena was not so eager. She came over and hugged me and kissed me. I was afraid that I'd cry and make a fool of myself, but I didn't.

I walked around to the far side of the car with her, where nobody could see except maybe Pa, and I gave her a parcel.

"What's this?" she said. "A love letter?"

"No," I said. "It's our alphabet chart. All finished. I thought you might use it—to learn . . . to teach Micky how to . . ." but she bent down and kissed me before I could finish.

My last sight of the children was through the rear window of the station wagon. They didn't wave. Their fingers gripped the bars of the metal grille that was fitted there.

twenty-four

Julia left for school two weeks later. She had five hundred times more things to pack than Leena. She filled two of her new suitcases with uniforms alone: Summer uniforms, winter uniforms, sports uniforms, summer blouses, winter blouses, a blazer, a pullover, a cardigan, a tie, a scarf, regulation underwear, shoes, socks, stockings . . .

"Look at that ugly thing," she said, pointing to a drab gray pinafore laid out on her bed. "It's like a suit of armor. Look at the bodice. . . ."

She picked it up.

"Double-breasted, for heaven's sake. Isn't that a joke! The whole idea of it is to *suppress* the breasts, not *double* them! And these are 'box pleats' . . . 'box pleats' would you believe! Why not 'coffin pleats'? That's what they look like. A whole row of coffins, all dangling around your legs . . . clunk, clunk . . . 'And remember girls, we must be careful to keep them perfectly pressed' . . . that's what the headmistress says—Miss Fluggwart, or whatever her name is."

I felt sorry for Julia, especially not having a room of her own. "What will you do when the others snore and fart?" I asked her. "I'd hate it."

"I won't be sleeping with them that much," she said, busily tugging at a cardigan to stretch it out of shape.

I thought that she must have misunderstood. "At night, I meant. In the dormitory."

She gave me a penetrating look. "Can you be trusted yet?" she said.

I refused to answer.

She called me closer and sat me down on the bed beside her. "I've been busting to tell you. I've got a job."

"What kind of a job?"

She sat back a little and examined me through half-closed eyes. "This is a big deal. Can you really . . ."

"Yes, I *can* keep a secret," I said. "You'd be surprised. Now go on."

"Well, before I went down with Momsie for our visit to the school, I dropped in to see Ruby—and asked her for a reference. 'Certainly,' she said. Then I asked her if she had any contacts in the big hotels down the coast. She did. She's a very good friend of the manager of the Mayfair. And where do you think we stayed when we went down?"

I was starting to get the picture. "Julia," I said, "you're crazy."

She took no notice. "So . . . when Momsie had a nap before dinner, I paid the manager a visit. I'd say he was a very, very good friend of Ruby's. 'Ruby Parsons?' he said. 'Not my Ruby? Not my Jericho Ruby? She sent you? That's a good enough recommendation for me.'"

"What about school?" I protested. "You have to go to school."

She returned to stretching her cardigan. "Not at night, I don't. Not if I'm a night maid at the Mayfair from ten till six."

"You're going to sneak out of the dorm?"

"Only three nights a week. Tuesdays, Wednesdays, and Thursdays. It shouldn't be too hard. I'm not worried."

"Someone will tell," I said.

"No they won't." She was still destroying her cardigan.

"But if they do you'll get expelled."

"Good," she said. "So I win both ways."

Her bags were sent down the day before she left. After that she wandered around the house, looking here and there, just as she had on the last day of school.

That same afternoon, when my mother was busy in the kitchen, I caught Julia in the reception room calling a cab.

There was only one cab in Jericho, owned and driven by a man known simply as Little John. He was called this because he was the smallest adult male I'd ever seen. Even when he sat on a specially constructed car seat his view of the road was still through the steering wheel, not over it. Until the dam was begun, Little John had spent most of his days dozing behind the wheel or doing crosswords, but afterward he made a fortune driving drunks back to their quarters at the dam.

"Where are you going in a cab?" I said.

She grabbed me by the shoulders and squeezed me hard. "Don't you say a word, you little snoop," she hissed.

"I can't if I don't know what you're doing, can I?" I said. "But since it's your last day, it wouldn't hurt to tell. . . ."

She let me go. "Sorry," she said. "I'm just not myself. . . ."

She led me into the yard. "Don't say anything, not to them, but I'm going to see Bobby. It's something I want to do before I go. That's what I rang Little John for. He's picking me up down the hill and running me out there."

"That'll cost you a fortune," I warned, speaking entirely from hearsay.

"I've still got money from working at Ruby's. Anyway, I don't care. Friendship's more important than money."

I was amazed. "I thought it was all over between you and Bobby."

We had reached the vegetable patch. She said, "Remember that day we had to dig a hole and bury those blue parrots? The ones Flannagan brought in?"

I remembered.

"Do you remember what you said when they were in the bottom of the hole?"

"I wanted to know if they were a pair."

"And I said, 'They might be, like us.'" She sighed. "I've been thinking about a few things lately. Remembering things. It's Leena and Micky got me going. Seeing her with him; holding him like she did. And then the other night, I couldn't sleep thinking about Maureen Peed and that Ben Cullen. Now that was a pair, hey? And we still don't know what happened to her. She might have gone over that bridge, you know, or she might have gone right the way down the coast and been picked up by some millionaire. Then I thought about me and Bobby." She slipped this in quickly, almost as if I wasn't supposed to notice. "But that relationship wasn't going anywhere. He's too much of a farm boy for me."

"I don't think so," I said, surprising myself. I told her what Bobby told me when we were up at the Thumbs, about selling the farm and going back to school.

"You're pulling my leg, aren't you?" she said. "You're kidding me."

"I'm not, I promise."

"Well then, I'm glad that I decided to see him. I really am."

When I thought about it, I was too.

Next morning at breakfast Julia announced that she wouldn't be driven down to boarding school, as planned. She would be catching the bus alone.

My mother was furious. "I'm taking you and that's that."

"Then I won't go," Julia said flatly.

My mother dropped the breakfast dishes on the table, breaking one clean through. "Now look what you've made me do! I thought we were over all this rubbish. I thought that we'd sorted all this out."

"It is over, Mom; I'm not fighting you." She picked up the broken dishes.

My father appeared in the doorway.

"I'm listening," he said.

"I don't want Mom to drive me to school. I want to go alone. Like a grown-up."

"Yes," he said, "and what else? I know you. There's always something else."

"I want you to open the front gate. I want to walk straight out and down the hill. I want you all to stay in here, inside the house. No stupid good-byes."

She lifted her head and looked my father in the eye. "You'll do that for me, won't you, Dad?"

At ten o'clock, with the three of us waiting in the living room, I heard the click of stilettos on the stairs and, sure enough, right there before our eyes, Julia came down in her silver shoes and red dress.

"I'm ready," she said.

When my parents let me go, I climbed into the eyrie.

I looked out at the hills. A touch of sun lit the distant Thumbs. I remembered the fourth peak, hidden behind.

The west wind swept in through the Angel's Gate, cooling my face. Turning toward it, I lifted my arms. As I did, I heard a voice call from far away, "Would you fly, Kimmy? Would you?"

J CRE
Crew, Gary, 1947-
Angel's gate

J CRE
Crew, Gary, 1947-
Angel's gate